SKELETONS

SKELETONS

SHIMEKA R MCFADDEN

Six Kids & A Pen Publishing

All rights reserved.

Copyright © 2011 Shimeka Anderson

Cover Designed by Davida Baldwin at OddBall Design
www.oddballdsgn.com

Richard Bach Quote
www.thinkexist.com

This book may not be reproduced in whole or in part, in any form or by an electronic or mechanical means, including information storage and retrieval systems, without permission by the publisher, except by reviewers or catalogues no limited to online for purpose of promotion. For information address:

Six Kids & A Pen Publishig
Shimeka McFadden
1401 S Rodgers
Alton, IL 62002

www.sixkidsandapen.blogspot.com

This book is a work of fiction. Names, characters, places and incidental are either a product of fiction or are used in a fictious manner. Any resemblance to actual persons, living or dead, events, or locales is entirely coincidental.

ISBN: 978-0-615-49675-7

PRINTED IN THE UNITED STATES OF AMERICA

Acknowledgments

I would like to acknowledge my husband Kerri for enduring this six year journey with me as I wrote and revised Skeletons and to thank him for keeping me from hitting the delete button on many occasions. I would also like to thank my beautiful children, Takeyha, Asa, Peaceful, Javier, Boston and Januari for learning to like take out dinners, a messy house and a irritable mother while I prepped this book for publishing. I would like to say thank you to my sisters Tiffany and and Takeisha for having the understanding and love that only a sister can give. I would also like to thank my friends Artura, Chevon, Rachel, Erica, Loretta and Janita for all of your support and listening to me ramble on and on for hours and for over looking my bipolar moments. Last but not least I'd like to thank my parents, David and Donnia for allowing me to be who I am and for combining their DNA to create a very unique individual.

Thank you!

"The worst lies are the lies we tell ourselves. We live in denial of what we do, even what we think. We do this because we're afraid. We fear we will not find love, and when we find it we fear we'll lose it. We fear that if we do not love we will be unhappy."
Richard Bach 1936

1
JOVANNA

I hate Mondays.
Looking at me through pleading eyes Justin let out a heavy sigh as I pulled the red and black skull cap over my shoulder-length hair and pulled on the matching gloves. I hated when we fought, but I was determined to let him know that I was right.
"Are you ready?" he grunted as he grabbed the handle of my heavy Samsonite suitcase.
"There is no need for you to drive me to the airport Justin, I'm a big girl now and I'm sure that I can handle some things on my own."
Sighing, he said, "Jovanna, you know that I am not about to let you drive to the airport alone. In the five years of our being together I have never let you drive to the airport alone so what makes you think that I will now."
Rolling my brown eyes I yanked my heavy laptop bag up and walked out of the door without another word as Justin walked behind me with my suitcase in tow.
The ride down highway 170 to highway 70 there were no words between us, just the sounds of Musiq Soulchild singing sweet falsetto praises on how beautiful his woman is. Justin drove carefully down the highway because the roads were still slick from the snow storm that we

had the other day and he didn't want to risk crashing his tuxedo black Ford Super Duty truck. I could tell that he was still agitated from the conversation that we had last night by the way that he kept looking over at me, but knowing that it was in his best interest to keep quiet.
Pulling out my iPhone I called my assistant, Tony, who was already at the gate.
"Good morning, we are in route to the airport, but the streets are pretty bad so we are taking our time."
"Good morning sunshine," he sang back, "You don't have to tell me, I know how St. Louis is about cleaning the highway after a snowstorm. I was not about to bring my baby out in this mess so I took a cab."
"I am on my way, but did you confirm with Qwin's publicist and manager that we will be at B.E.D at noon tomorrow??"
"Yes doll." Tony said.
B.E.D is an exclusive lounge in South Beach that had beds for patrons to sit and lounge on instead of the usual tables and chairs. Since Qwin was turning twenty-one I decided to host the event there for a more sensual and upscale event rather than a hyped up club scene in New York. Qwin has been the artist of the year since he came out with his hit single, Bohemian Seduction. While I didn't listen to his music, I was relieved to hear I was not hosting another party for a rapper because their parties tended to get out of control and I was tired of having my name attached to those types of events.
"Okay, I'm going to be on his manager by ten because I don't want to get behind schedule."
"Yes mother." Tony chimed, "This is going to be a long three days honey."
I sighed and looked at Justin and said "I know."
After hanging up with Tony, Justin turned Musiq down and said, "Look Jovanna, I don't like us not talking and you know that."
I kept my gaze out of the window as if I were focusing on the snow.
"I don't know what I did that was so wrong; I swear sometimes your period makes you crazy."
I turned and looked into his blue eyes with heat in my brown ones, "Don't you even go there Justin." I stabbed. "Don't blame your insensitivity on my hormones."
"How am I being insensitive?"
"Do you realize that the wedding is in five months Justin and it is kind of disconcerting when my soon-to-be husband refuses to help me with the favors, the cake, the musical selection or the seating arrangement for the reception?" I shot.
Uncomfortable with being put on the spot Justin rubbed his goatee,

Skeletons

and said "That is not being insensitive, that is what we are paying a wedding coordinator for."

"These are personal touches that I don't want Trisha to make." I huffed.

"Why are we paying her then?" He asked. "You have planned hundreds of weddings so if you want to plan your own wedding then let's get a refund from Trisha."

I rolled my eyes, "I knew that you wouldn't understand."

"When I pay a contractor to flip a house for me, I don't go in and lay down the flooring because that is what I'm paying him for." he said in his New York accent.

"What are you talking about Justin? Are you really prepared to compare our wedding, the most important day or our lives, to your job of flipping houses?"

Justin's back was in a corner, "That is not what I'm saying Jovanna."

"That is what just came out of your damn mouth!" I shot quickly, "So clarify what you meant!"

Justin could see that I was angry.

"First of all, cursing me isn't necessary and secondly I didn't mean what I said in a way to demean our wedding or our marriage. You were the one who said that you were not going to coordinate our wedding because you were under enough stress so I assumed that you paid Trisha to handle all of the wedding details and all we did was say write a check, show up and say I do. I never intended to have to pick out party favors or make a seating chart, but if that is what you want then I will help you. I just don't want to fight."

Giving in Justin turned Musiq back up.

Looking at my pale, soon-to-be husband who was badly in need of a tan, I smiled and turned my gaze back to the highway taking comfort in the fact that he was worried about my stress level and not trying to skip out on helping with our wedding.

"Justin, I do this for a living and I just want our day to be just as special as everyone else's day. Just help me with the seating chart because I know how your family feels about our union and I don't want my friends to be subjected to their hateful scowls during my reception." I said softly as we continued our ride to the airport.

Tony looked as handsome as ever in a pair of antique washed black jeans and a thick sweater and tied it all together with a pageboy cap and ebony pea coat as he waved to us in front of the luggage rack; Justin laughed "Wow for once he doesn't have on every color of the rainbow." I have to admit Tony was eccentric in his dress, usually wearing something that let people know who he was, what he was and that there was no shame in his game. However, Tony knew how to separate business from pleasure so when we were conducting business he was always on point and made sure that he was dressed to impress.
"It's about damn time." He said as he took my suitcase from Justin. "Hey Justin how are you?"
"I'm fine Tony, I almost didn't recognize you."
Tony laughed, "Yeah I had to tone it down for these bitches in South Beach, but honey I still got it." He said adjusting his cap.
Justin laughed, "Jovanna, call me when you get to your hotel."
"I always do Justin." I smiled, relieved to have put this argument behind us.
Justin kissed me softly on the lips and shook Tony's hand, "Take care of my lady, she is all that I got." He said before he walked out of the airport.
"Girl you got him whipped like cool whip." Tony joked as we walked to the security check. "But I must say that Justin is one fine white man!"
"Keep your mitts off of my fiancé you whore." I laughed.
Standing in line I pulled out my iPhone to send a text to my girls, Santana and Asteria:
Hey ladies, just wanted to let you know that I'm about to get on the plane headed to South Beach for the 21st birthday bash for Qwin and I will be back in St. Louis Wednesday evening, but you know that I'll always be with you in spirit and via text.
Kisses

2
SANTANA

Monday morning and we are running late as usual.

Reading Jovanna's text pissed me off even more; as we rushed around the house trying to get out of the door, she was headed to the warmth of South Beach to throw a party for that young fine ass new artist, Qwin. While I love my job as Senior CPA for Gold's Medical Supply, I envied the life that Jovanna lived; she was always mingling with celebrities or hosting one of the most talked about events, I think that I am in the wrong line of work.

"Malik and Mya let's go!" I yelled from the bottom of the stairs at my twelve-year-old son and nine year-old daughter who were taking their own sweet time to get out of the door.

Michael, my husband, walked into the kitchen with a frantic look on his face, which usually meant that he couldn't find something. Grabbing his coffee cup off of the island he tried to take a sip, but ended up spilling coffee on his suit as he too was in a hurry to get to work.

"Have you seen the keys to my car?" he asked as he fumbled with a cup of hot coffee in one hand, his briefcase in another while trying to clip on his lackluster blue tie. I just shook my head. Michael felt that he could not operate without his morning cup of coffee every day, even on the weekends.

I grabbed my purse and the keys to my van as I tried to help him look for his set of keys, "Where did you have them last Mike?"

"I don't remember."

It always seemed to amaze me how my husband could manage an entire call center with over two hundred employees, but couldn't manage to keep up with his car keys.

"I keep telling you to put your keys on the key holder when you come in the door." I fussed with my hand on my ample hips.

Mike looked at me blankly and said, "Well that is kind of a moot point, don't you think Santana?"

Rolling my eyes I called for the kids once more, "Let's go, you two have ten seconds to get your butts down here or you will be left to walk to school in the snow!"

Malik, my handsome caramel-skinned son walked in first zipping his book bag and grabbing his lunch from the island counter. "I'm ready, but I can't find my iPod."

Sighing, I grabbed his blue iPod from off of the top of the refrigerator, "This was left on the island last night. What have I told you about putting your things away?"

"Thanks." he said as he checked the battery power on it.

Mya skipped in the kitchen, her braids swaying with her movement, "I'm ready mom."

Mike walked in the room frantic, "Kids have you seen my keys?"

"Dad you left them in your bathroom." Malik said, "I used some of your cologne and I just saw them sitting there."

Mike ran back upstairs to our bathroom.

"What did your daddy tell you about using his cologne without his permission?"

Malik shrugged as he walked out of the door behind Mya.

The kid's school was only a five minute drive from our house in Barrington Downs, but today it seemed that people wanted to drive slower than normal. I turned on Grand National Drive when I almost rear-ended a woman who was too busy talking on her cellular phone to see that I had the right a way.

"Dumb bitch!" I yelled as I laid on my horn.

"Mommy just used a bad word." Mya corrected me from the back seat. "Daddy said that God' doesn't like bad words."

"Not today Mya, mommy is stressed enough." I said, "Did you grab your book report from off the dining room table?"

"Yes mom."

"Mom, do you think that I can go to De`Vante's house after school today?" Malik asked.

"You have been spending a lot of time over his house lately; what are the two of you up to?"

"Just hanging out and playing video games since I can't have a Playstation of my own like a normal kid."

"Daddy said that video games are too violent and not Christian-like." Mya sang.

"Did De'Vante ask Pam about this?" I asked ignoring my daughter.

"Yes and she said that it was okay and that she'd drive me home by seven o'clock."

"Alright, but call me as soon as you get over there."

"You don't trust me?"

"Malik, just call me when you get over there, it's not about trust, it's about knowing that you are alright."

After dropping the kids off at school I made my way down the highway as I frantically tried to avoid the rest of the manic drivers on the road while cursing MODOT for not having the streets cleaned by now. As I pulled into the parking garage my phone lit up, it was my new assistant, Tabitha.

"I'm in the parking lot Tabitha." I said clearly irritated by the call.

"Mr. Gold and Mr. Berganstein are expecting you in this meeting and I want to make sure that you are not late."

"I'm running late, but I'm going to be in the meeting on time." I said as I grabbed the finance reports out of my briefcase and power-walked to the elevator up to the tenth floor of our building. While I didn't have the exciting job that Jovanna had it more than paid the bills and allowed me a lot of free time off to be with the family so I put up with it.

Shimeka R. McFadden

3
ASTERIA

Bring me some of that good South Beach weather back! Love you.
Asteria

I typed Jovanna a reply as I began my day at Gods & Goddesses Salon where I work as business manager and co-owner with my twin sister Pandia. Our mother was a Greek mythology buff and thought that it was cute to name us after Grecian Goddesses. While I didn't know a lot about Greek mythology I did my research and found out that Asteria was the Goddess of night and falling stars and Pandia was the Goddess of light and beauty. Just like our names, Pandia and I were like night and day.

I always got into the salon before any of the other stylists because I liked to make sure everyone's station was fully stocked and clean before we started our day. Pandia fusses at me saying that I spoil the stylist and that it was not my job to stock and clean their stations. However, I wanted the stylist at their stations and ready to work when they came into the salon; it was not productive to have them running around looking for this and that while a client was in the chair. Besides after dropping my son off at daycare, I didn't have anything else to keep me busy.

My sister, who has no business sense, is used to working at salons where the stylist popped gum in the client's ear, talked about everybody's business except their own while rap music blared in the background and the stylists had messy stations. When we decided to open Gods & Goddesses Salon we agreed that this was going to be an upscale shop that ran like a finely tuned automobile instead of a jalopy.

Pandia was not use to the business end of things; while my womb-mate was going to beauty school, I was busy hitting the books at UMSL ultimately obtaining my Bachelor's Degree in Business and Professional Development and moving to Phoenix to work for a prestigious business consultant.

I moved back to St. Louis when my mother was diagnosed with breast cancer. Since Pandia was trying to run a salon, tend to her son and deal with her philandering husband I moved home to help her with mom. While I loved my mother she always seemed to favor Pandia over me. No matter how much I achieved and she underachieved, mom held a special place in her heart for my sister, a spot that I never got a chance to see. While I was busy making high-honor roll and a member of minority excellence in high school, mom was praising Pandia for making the cheerleading squad. When I made captain of the track team with very little fanfare, mom took Pandia shopping for getting an A on her science project on the solar system. Even when Pandia married Keith the smile on mom's face was one filled with love and admiration a look that I didn't get to see even after I graduated with my Bachelor's degree.

On mom's death bed I asked her why didn't she love me as much as she loved my sister. All mom said was, "Asteria, you are just like your father, always thinking that there is a competition when you are clearly the one winning the race." She passed away peacefully in her sleep a few weeks after, but I never forgot the words that she spoke to me. Her final insult came when we went over the life insurance policy and learned that Pandia got eighty percent and I was left with only twenty. After her funeral we took the remaining money from the policy and opened up the salon in University City.

After stocking the stations I went to the front desk and booted up the computer to print out everyone's schedule for the day. Gods & Goddesses stayed so heavily book that we had no choice but to open every other Monday while most salons were closed. A client had to book three weeks in advance for a hair weave and we housed some of the best stylists and barbers in St. Louis.

Aaron was always first in, he was sexy with his honey coated skin, light brown eyes, shoulder length dreadlocks and lips that would make LL drool, and too bad he was as sweet as grandma's Kool-Aid.

"Hey chica!" he smiled at me as he walked towards his station; Aaron is one of the best locticians in the area. "How was your date Saturday night?" I asked as I handed him his schedule.

He scratched the raised scar that ran from the corner of his left eye down to his full lips. He never told me the story behind the scar, but I knew that he carried a blade with him wherever he went.

"Now you know that Aaron don't kiss and tell."

"So you did kiss though?" I teased.

Aaron blew me an air kiss and walked to the break room.

Keisha, walked in with her usual bad attitude and without speaking she looked over her schedule in disgust. We put up with her attitude because she was fresh out of beauty school and he was a good stylist.

"Good morning." I smiled.

"Hi." she said dryly while sitting down in her stylist chair with a frown on her face. "Why do I always get stuck with the shitty schedule?"

"What are you talking about Keisha?" I asked.

"Everyone else gets their own clients and I always get stuck with the non-regulars and walk-ins. What's up with that?" she tossed the paper on the glass-topped station.

"Keisha, you are the low man on the totem pole and you haven't built up a clientele yet so those are the breaks. Besides you haven't been here long enough so have

a little patience. In the meantime you need to sharpen your skills and work on your professionalism and maybe you will start to build your clientele up."

Rolling her counterfeit grey eyes hidden behind thick imitation lashes she began picking her nails. Pandia hated Keisha and her funky approach, but I saw potential in her so I opted to keep her on staff.

Next was my very own Sista-Big-Bones, Londyn, don't get it twisted Londyn was a hefty sista with more class, soul and ass than any one that I've ever met. Today she wore a pair of winter white wide-legged pants, chocolate brown Kenneth Cole leather boots with a thin four-inch heel and a chocolate brown sweater straight from AshleyStewart.com. She was gabbing away on her cell phone as she walked in the door, I handed her the days schedule and with a friendly wave she sashayed back to her station, making sure to stop her conversation long enough to say "Good morning Keisha." to Keisha and continue her conversation and her catwalk back to her space.

My cellular vibrated, it was Pandia who was running late again.

"Pandia you have a client due in at nine-thirty, do you think that you can make it in by then?" I answered.

"Don't talk to me like you own me Asteria." she fussed, "Keith didn't make it in until late last night so I have to drop little Keith off at school and now we are stuck in traffic."

Sounding suprised I asked, "Where in the hell was he?"

"The hell if I know, but I do know that I'm getting real tired of this bullshit."

I could hear the hurt in her voice.

"Well, shit or get off of the pot is what mom use to say."

"Yeah, it is easy for you to tell me to get rid of my husband when you don't have a clue of what it is to be married."

"Wow that was a bit below the belt." I said pretending to be hurt.

"I'm sorry, I'm just sick of this. I will be there when I can."

"We have a full schedule today, Pandia so if your first client is left waiting for more than ten minutes I'll have to pass her to Keisha."

"No! Don't do that, Mrs. Alexander is very particular about her hair and she'd have a fit if that little girl messes her up."

"Well unless you get here in time, I don't have a choice because everyone has a full schedule except for Keisha. Besides she is a good stylist Pandia, in business you have to learn to set aside your personal feelings for someone in order to grow professionally."

"Whatever, tell her to wash her hair and put her under the dryer, by that time I should be there."

"Alright, I will see you when you get here." I said with a smile on my face.

4
JOVANNA

No matter how many times we've been to South Beach and have stayed at Hotel Victor we still had a hassle when we checked in, but I refused to stay anywhere else. I am always blown away be the modern décor and the ultra-chic vibe that circulated throughout the luxury hotel. As usual the beautiful, but inept girl at the front desk couldn't find our reservation, even though we had the confirmation number. Tony's eyes lit up when he saw the cute hotel manager come to her aid. Not only did we walk away with many apologies, but also complementary breakfast for the duration of our trip and Tony got the managers phone number.
"You are something else Tony." I laughed shaking my head as my business partner typed the manager's phone number into his Evo.
"Girl you have to learn how to go after the things that you want in life, besides I'm single and ready to mingle in South Beach." he switched as we got on the elevator.
I yawned.
"Damn it was only a three hour flight and you are tired already."
"I know, that is all that I have been doing lately is sleeping. I don't know what is going on with me."
"Maybe it's the stress from all of that planning that you have been doing

for this lavish wedding that you have coming up."
"Justin pissed me off so bad last night."
"Get over that shit, you got you a good Caucasian man!" he laughed.
"Stop Tony, I'm serious." I swatted him on his arm.
"Has his family opened up to you yet? I know that his rich, white family does not want him to marry the likes of us." He said holding up the back of his brown hand.
"It is not their decision to make and Justin and I are fine with that." I answered as I adjusted the heavy bag on my shoulder.
"Whatever, get dressed hooker, I want to head to this new club that I read about." He said grabbing his bags off of the cart and stepping off of the elevator.
"You go ahead without me tonight, I have some work to do and you need to make sure that our vendors are in place."
"Don't worry about my end; you know that I have got this." He switched to his room.
I had the final count for the V.I.P guest list and make sure that the owner of B.E.D knew to open the venue up for the vendors a few hours in advance, but first I had to take a shower.
Closing my eyes while the hot water ran down my tense body melting away the stress in my muscles. This wedding was stressing me out and I couldn't wait to say "I do" and jump on a plane for Tokyo for a much needed two week vacation. Running my hands down the lather that slid down my body the lavender scent of the soap engulfed my senses in an attempt to relax me even more. Losing that extra twenty pounds by picking up running again really helped my physique; I had muscles in places where I didn't even know they existed. My deep chocolate abs were beginning to get more formed and taut, my legs were so toned that they no longer jiggled when I ran and my ass was firm and tight, but still had a little bounce to it when I needed it to.
Justin has always loved my body, but he appreciates it even more now that I've been working out. Trying to get Santana and Asteria to lose an hour of sleep to run with me was like pulling teeth so I've gotten into the habit of running with my man or alone when he is out of town on business.
Meeting Justin was one of the best moments of my life only coming second to me moving from having nothing in Memphis to running, Elite Events by Jovanna, my own event coordinating company. Justin was not the first white man that I'd been with, but he was the first white man that I ever kissed and the first man that I ever felt truly loved me.
I thought that Justin was too good to be true, I've never had a man treat

me with such kindness and care. He was genuine, sincere and most importantly he treated me with respect. I had a wall up, a wall that was built with many bricks of my past, but Justin worked to break away the bricks one by one earning my trust enough for me to fall in love with him.

Santana and Asteria thought that it was funny during our first year of dating, we were the butt of every joke at all of the functions and barbeques; during year two, they said that it was just a phase and it would pass; by year three they were angry that I'd chosen a white man instead of a good black man, but by year four they began to accept Justin as a part of our circle and now, five years later they were looking forward to stand beside us as we took our vows in front of God.

Justin's family has been a major roadblock in our relationship, they knew that Justin preferred African American women, but they were confident that their son was smart enough not to marry one. His mother, who was a recovering alcoholic, almost fell off the wagon when he announced that we were engaged. His father, Rick, was absolutely pissed off that his son was dating an African American and the heir to his last name would have black blood running though his veins. They sneered at me when Justin would bring me to holiday celebrations eventually it got so bad that I stopped going with him and soon thereafter Justin stopped attending as well.

Although I made it my point to send his family invitations to our wedding, we were prepared for them not to show. I knew that he hurt Justin not being able to connect with his family as he once did, but he loved me and told them that they would either have to accept our union or accept him not being part of their lives any longer.

I stepped out of the shower and wrapped the plush terry cloth bath robe around my body and stepped out onto the balcony. The warm air felt good on my damp skin and the smell of the ocean took me back to when I first visited South Beach, but at that time it was on the other side of the tracks and the memories are not something that I wanted to recall. Hearing my cell phone chime in my room took me back to reality as I went inside to answer the call.

"Hello."

"What are you wearing?" Justin said trying to sound as sexy as his thick New York accent would allow.

"Justin, what do you want?"

"Come on, play along with me." He said. "Now what are you wearing?"

I tried to keep my laugh in, "I'm wearing a hot pink lace thong and matching tank top."

"Is it see through?"
"Yes, baby they are both sheer."
Justin moaned, "Can you see those brown nipples through the tank top?"
"Yes baby." I breathed, "You can see the imprint of my pussy through my panties too." I looked at the time, it was only two-thirty in St. Louis and Justin was still at work.
"Damn, I bet that is a very sexy sight."
"It is baby and I just got out of the shower so my skin smells sweet and feels so soft. I wish that you were here to touch and to taste me baby." I purred into my phone as I looked for the seating arrangements in my briefcase.
"Touch yourself for me." He demanded.
Rolling my eyes at his request, I had too much shit on my plate to play phone sex with Justin. I moaned into the ear piece as I pretended to caress my body. "I wish that you were here to do this for me."
"I just want to watch you." Justin was a freaky little white boy.
"Are you wet?"
"Yes."
"Does it feel good to you?"
I moaned.
"Touch your breasts for me."
"I am baby, I am." I moaned.
"Damn you are turning me on."
I don't know why he wants to be at work rock hard, but Justin was really into phone sex.
"I am about to come baby." I moaned and panted into the phone, "I can't hold back any longer."
"Come for me, make that cherry melt baby."
I moaned and panted harder and louder as I pretended to orgasm and ended it with me screaming his name over and over again—my performance was Oscar worthy.
I could hear Justin's breathing deepen, then he suddenly stopped short, "I'm sorry, but I think that I have the wrong number." He said, ending the call.
Justin has made it a habit to call me for phone sex when either of us was out of town and even though I thought it was silly, I did it to make him happy.
The following morning Tony and I met in the lobby of the hotel for breakfast then we took a taxi to B.E.D in order to meet with Qwin and his people for a final meeting and payment before the party. I was suprised

at how short Qwin was compared to what he looked like in his videos, but I knew how clever cameramen could be with shooting smaller men from below in order to make them look larger. I learned not to trust the cameras after going to a DMX concert some time ago.

As I went over the plans for the party with him and his manager were busy talking to the owner of B.E.D to let him know what time the vendors would start showing up tomorrow to decorate and get the place set up.

"I'm sorry that I'm late." Someone said from behind me, turning around I did not stumbled when I saw a familiar face that I hadn't expected to see ever again.

With an extended hand the dark haired brick house introduced herself as Qwin's publicist, Tasha.

"Wow, it is nice to finally meet you." I smiled shaking her hand.

With familiarity in her green eyes she said, "It is nice to put a face behind a voice."

We knew one another, and she was not who she said she was.

"I was just explaining to Qwin and Mr. Tomlinson that he will make his entrance from the left behind a set of sheer red curtains." I explained pointing to the area while trying to regain my composure.

"Okay sounds good."

After explaining the details of the party to the group I left them alone to discuss any further details that they needed me to know and I sat at the bar next to Tony who was on the phone with the caterer.

"What's wrong love, you look like you've seen a ghost." He asked.

"Nothing, I guess I'm still a bit jet lagged." I lied, "How is everything going with the vendors?" I asked.

"It's all good, I've changed a few menu items, but I doubt that they will realize it."

"Just make sure you give me the final price when you are done." I said as I looked up to see Tasha headed my way.

"Everything sounds great, Jovanna and here is your check." She said handing me a check.

Checking the amount I thanked her and walked the trio to the door.

Shaking Qwin and his manager's hand I told them that I'd see them tomorrow night for the party. Before leaving Tasha turned to back to me and smiled, "You look good."

Pretending not to know what she was talking about, "Excuse me."

"Don't worry I won't say anything, I just wanted you to know that you look good and it was nice seeing you again."

"How do you remember me?" I asked after making sure that I was out of earshot of anyone else.

"I have a good memory. I always wondered what happened to you and now that I see that you are doing well, I feel much better."
"I try not to think about it."
"It is hard not to think about it."
"You look good too, Tasha." I smiled.
Embracing me she whispered, "Don't worry, your secret is safe with me." With a soft kiss on my cheek she entered her rented Benz and drove off leaving me feeling exposed.

5
SANTANA

The migraine had taken over my mood as I sat in my office staring at the monthly expense report on my desk. I tossed the report to the side and leaned back in the leather chair closing my eyes trying to relax. Jovanna was one lucky bitch to be in South Beach in the middle of a Midwestern winter while the rest of us were stuck in cold, snowy St. Louis. Even though we gave her a hard time about marrying Justin, I was happy that she found someone to love her. Mike and I use to be in love, but lately it felt more like we were just going through the motions of being married. We'd been together since high school, before we even knew who we really were, and I think that was the problem between us now. We didn't know who we were without one another; I was always Mike's Santana and he was always my Mike.

Tabitha rushed into my office, her four inch stilettos clicking on the hardwood floor as she moved, "Hey, sorry that it took me so long, but the line was crazy at Walgreens today." She said handing me the pills. "How are you feeling?"

I frowned, "I'll be fine."

Tabitha sat in the chair in front of my desk crossing her thick thighs, she sure knew how to wear a skirt. I wondered how many heads she turned at Walgreens. I smiled.

"What's wrong?"

Shaking my head as I swallowed the pills, "Nothing, I was just thinking."

"Do you need to take a personal day Santana because you are starting to scare me?"

"No, I am fine Tab; did Glenda get you those receipts yet?" I asked.

"She said that she'd get them to us today after lunch."

"I don't understand why it takes her the longest to get the receipts up here to us. Everyone knows that they have to be turned in on the twelfth of every month and yet I always have to wait on her." I fussed as I rubbed the back of my neck, "I can't do my job unless she does her job."

"Would you like for me to send an email requesting all receipts need to be in our office on the twelfth working day of the month with no exceptions?"

"Yes, go ahead and do that."

"Did you and Mike get out this weekend?"

I rolled my eyes at the question, "Girl please."

"You two act like you are an elderly couple." She giggled, "Live a little!"

"What did you get into?"

Tabitha threw her long brown weave over her shoulders, "We went to The Loft on Friday night, I had a breakfast date Saturday morning, Saturday night I got together with the girls for drinks at The Melting Pot and from there we headed to The Drunken Fish to hang out, eat sushi and drink sake."

"What time did you get home?"

"I got home last night because we all slept over at Natasha's house until after four in the evening then we went to dinner and from there I picked up my car at the Metro Link station and went home."

"I don't see how you do it girl."

"Do what?" she laughed that carefree way that most twenty-six year old, single, childless women laughed, "That was mild."

"Did you meet any guys?" I asked with a raised eyebrow.

As usual she shrugged her shoulders and simply said, "No."

I didn't understand Tabitha, she was a beautiful girl with smooth, flawless dark skin, big brown eyes and a body that would make Beyoncé have to step her game up yet she was single. Tabitha wore nothing but designer clothes and shoes, carried the latest designer bags on the market and drove a nicer car than I did, all on an assistant's salary. It just didn't add up; maybe someone's man was taking care of her and she had to keep it on the down low.

"You should come out with us sometime Santana." She suggested.

I looked up for the expense report, "I don't want to be the old person in

Skeletons

the club." I laughed.

"You act like you are in your fifties Santana, you are only thirty-four-years old and you don't look a day over twenty seven." She smiled, "I'm serious you should come out with my friends and I one night."

"Okay, I'll think about it." I lied.

"Great, as a matter-of-fact we are all getting together for my birthday in two weeks and I'm going to be sure to send you an evite." She smiled as she rose up to leave, "Please don't stand me up." She winked and switched out of my office door.

I'd forgotten all about my migraine until I looked at my cell phone and saw that I had a text message from Mike

Have you seen my Blackberry?

Rolling my eyes I texted him back:

You left it on your night stand—remember me telling you to make sure that you didn't forget it this morning?

Hitting send I began trying to remember the last time Mike and I even touched one another in a passionate way, but I couldn't even remember. It is not like we have a bad relationship, but it just lacked passion, fire and desire. Before we had the kids and settled into this pseudo life we had enough passion to burn down the entire city of St. Louis and some of Chicago too. We were one another's first and only lover so everything was so new and we spent hours just exploring one another. I remember when we first got married we would go to bed together and wake the neighbors every night, but now I'm in bed by nine o'clock and he is in the den watching ESPN until after midnight. Sex has become more of a chore than a desire like cleaning out the refrigerator. We only had sex once a month if that and most of the time my mind is on planet Venus and his is on Mars—we were no longer connected.

"What are you doing for lunch?" Tabitha smiled as she poked her head into my office.

I looked up from my work and frowned, "I'm not sure, maybe I'll go to Subway and get a foot long."

She laughed, "Oh you are so boring, come have lunch with my girlfriend and I we are going to Charlie Gitto's."

"You're eating Charlie Gitto's for lunch?" I questioned, "No you two go ahead, I have some phone calls that I have to make during lunch and I'll ruin the hour."

"Come on, live a little, you can make those calls any time Santana." She urged.

"No, you two go ahead and go without me, maybe next time."

Tabitha let out a heavy sigh before she turned to leave.

Shimeka R. McFadden

I really didn't have any phone calls to make I just didn't want to go to lunch with two extremely beautiful, 20-something girls while I was a married woman in my thirties. Watching the men drool over their every move while they barely noticed me while I sat back and look like their aunt who was giving them advice; that would've been torture.

While eating lunch, alone in my office I received a text message from Mike:

Please make me a dentist appointment, my tooth is killing me.

6
ASTERIA

Pandia finally arrived just after Keisha washed Mrs. Alexander's hair; I was working on inventory when she flew past me.
"Good morning Pandia." I said annoyed that she didn't bother to speak to anyone.
Pandia and I were twins, but we didn't look nor did act anything alike; she was short with plenty of curves like our mother, I on the other hand, take my height and athletic build from our father. We both were fair skinned with honey colored eyes like our mom, but Pandia opted to wear colored contacts whereas I did not.
I could tell that Pandia was having one hell of a day as she styled Mrs. Alexander's hair so I left her alone. I stepped out on the back patio and lit up a cigarette, leaned back and closed my eyes. Just as I began to relax, Keisha stepped out.
"Can I borrow one?" she asked pointing to my cigarettes.
I handed her one and my lighter then went back to relaxing.
"Why doesn't Pandia like me?" She asked matter-of-factly.
I opened my eyes, "How do you know that she dislikes you Keisha?"
She blew smoke, "I'm not stupid, everyone knows that she hates me, but I just don't understand why."
"She thinks that you are unprofessional, arrogant, lazy and that you

don't belong here." I said bluntly, "But I think that you are talented and with the right mentoring you will go far."

"How is she going to call me unprofessional when she brings her problems to work with her? I don't have any issues with Pandia, but I swear one day if she comes at me the wrong way…"

"Keisha, you can't let people get to you girl, you have to just do you and forget about what other people say or how they feel about you." I interjected.

Once again she blew smoke, "I am not who she thinks I am." She put her cigarette out and walked back into the salon.

Just as I was walking in behind her my cellular phone rang, it was from a private number and only one person called me private.

"Hello." I answered.

"Damn baby last night was amazing; I could barely make it out of bed this morning."

Smiling I said, "You better get your ass up and get to work, I'm not taking care of a man."

"Stop with all of that girl, I am on my way to the station now."

"You be careful out there Officer Stevens."

He moaned, "You know that I love it when you call me that. Girl you are going to make me turn this car around and come up there and fuck the shit out of you in one of those swiveling chairs."

"I dare you."

He got quiet for a minute, "Where is your sister?"

He never asked about Pandia.

"She is doing hair, why?"

"I was just wondering."

"She was pissed off this morning."

Sighing heavily he said, "Yeah, but damn baby you put it on me. I may have to wife you one day."

"Sounds like a plan." I smiled then Pandia walked out, "I have to get back to work; I'll talk to you soon."

"Who was that?" Pandia asked.

"Damn you nosey sis." I smiled as I handed her a cigarette.

I could see the sadness in her eyes; sitting next to her I put my arm around her as she leaned her head on my shoulder. "Tell me all about it." With tears in her eyes and heartbreak in her voice Pandia began to tell a story that I have heard many of times before; a story about how her husband was running around on her and how she was going to leave him and find her a new man that would treat her right. I sat and listened to every word she said all the while knowing that she was not going to

Skeletons

leave Keith, he would have to be the one to leave.

Shimeka R. McFadden

7
JOVANNA

Qwin's party was a success, the vendors showed up on time, the DJ had the music pumping, and people were on the dance floor dancing or in one of the beds mingling, and Qwin seemed to be enjoying his self while in one of the VIP suites surrounded by young ass and big breasts. I had to admit to myself that I pulled off an event that they would be talking about for a long time and this would put me even further on top of the game.
"Hey girl this party is off the chain!" Tasha came up to me dancing to the music.
"Thanks, how is Qwin enjoying himself?"
"Girl, with all of that ass in his face he is doing very well." She laughed. "They are in there making it rain, but I remember back in the day you use to make it thunder."
Shocked that she said that out loud I grabbed Tasha by the arm and pulled her close, "I am not that person anymore; I don't like to be reminded of those days."
"I'm sorry girl; I guess the Nuvo got me twisted." She laughed as she danced away.
While watching the party from the back of the room a waitress came up to me with a drink on her tray.

"This is for you." She said putting the drink in my hand.
"I'm sorry, but I didn't order anything."
"I know, but the gentleman at the bar told me to send you this on him." She said pointing past the crowded room towards the bar.
"What is this?" I asked.
"It's a Tom Collins." She yelled. "He said that it is your favorite drink the bartender has never heard of this before so we had to ask the gentleman how to make it." She laughed.
Grabbing the drink I stormed through the room looking for Tasha, she was the only person here who would've known that I use to drink Tom Collins. I found her in the VIP room with Qwin, grabbing her by the arm and pulling her to a corner I spat, "Is this your idea of a sick joke?"
Confused she yanked away from me, "What in the hell are you talking about?"
"The Tom Collins, you sent me this drink!" I fumed.
"I didn't send you shit, you are tripping."
"You didn't send me this drink?" I asked again showing her the drink.
"No, but I see that you still get down with Mr. Collins though."
Handing her the drink I stormed out of the room to find Tony who was sitting at the bar chatting up some man.
"Did you happen to send me a drink?" I asked.
"No doll, I know that you don't drink during an event." He said. "Why what's wrong?"
My eyes scanned the room as my heartbeat beat louder than the music, "Nothing, I'm just ready to go home." I answered with my eyes still scanning the crowd for a familiar face, a face that I knew I didn't want to see.
The next morning I began packing my bags when a knock came at the door.
"Good morning, I have a package for you." The concierge said handing me a white envelope.
Thinking that it was the final payment for the party I took the envelope and put it on the nightstand and went back to packing. I called Tony who was nursing a hangover and told him what time to meet me in the lobby.
"Yes mother." He moaned.
After hanging up with him I sent a text message to Santana and Asteria: *The party was the shit! Who throws the best parties in America? I DO! I'm tired and homesick, our plane leaves at twelve and I'll be back in STL by three-thirty. I'll call you when I get in.*
Love You!

Skeletons

Attaching two pictures from the party I sent the text message and walked out on the balcony for one last look at paradise. I walked back inside and picked up the envelope turning it over and almost losing my sanity when I read to whom it was addressed to: *MARQUITA*. Pulling the note out of the envelope I read the finely written letter: *YOU OWE ME.* Ripping the letter into shreds and flushing it down the toilet I picked up my phone and dialed Tasha's number.
"Listen you stupid bitch, I don't know what you are trying to do but I don't appreciate it!"
"What in the hell are you talking about Jovanna?"
"The drink last night, the letter today please don't act dumb."
"First of all, I told you last night that I didn't send you that drink and I'm telling you today that I didn't send you a drink and I didn't send you a letter." She shot, "It was not me."
"Who else knows about this?"
"I don't know, but it is not me!" she said then hung up.
Running into the bathroom, I vomited my complimentary breakfast into the toilet bowl. I couldn't get out of South Beach fast enough.

Shimeka R. McFadden

8
ASTERIA

Keith had the body of a Greek God, from his rock hard six pack to his legs that were as thick as tree trunks. It was well after midnight as I lay naked across my king-sized bed watching him dress.

"Baby are you sure that you can't stay the night?" I pouted, "Trust me there is more of what you just got to come." I spread my thighs.

Glancing my way he smiled, "Not tonight Asteria, I have to get home."

Huffing I got out of bed and slid a T-shirt over my naked body, "Why is she tripping again?"

He put on his black Timberland boots in silence.

"I'm getting tired of this Keith; I'm tired of giving, giving and giving yet feeling empty in return."

"Asteria, why do we always have to go through this when I can't spend the night with you?" He asked, "You know my situation better than anyone else."

Running my hand through my tangled hair I continued to pout, but softened when he came towards me; Keith was at least one foot taller than me so I had to strain my neck to look up at him.

"I promise that I will make it up to you real soon." He said as his full lips covered mine.

Shimeka R. McFadden

Kissing him felt so right, I know that Keith and I were destined to be together if only he weren't someone else's man. As we embraced I ran my hand along the tight muscles on his back until his phone vibrated. Looking at the display on his phone he looked at me with regret in his eyes, "I've got to…"

"Go." I said as I opened my bedroom door for him to make his usual late night exit.

Standing in the window I watched my midnight lover's truck pull out of my driveway, he was on his phone, most likely with her telling her how he was out with the boys and he lost track of time. She was a fool, how many times I'd heard him use that same tired ass line on her while he was lying in bed with me in his arms. How foolish she was for allowing him to come home with the smell of another woman's pussy on his dick and lips. While she stays home with their son he lays in the bed of his lover, my sister was a fool.

My love affair with Keith didn't start off as a love affair at all; actually we couldn't stand one another. Pandia introduced Keith to me while I was still in college and while I thought he was very attractive, I did not dig his cocky attitude. Keith and Pandia were as different as night and day, while she was the type to stay at home reading or watching movies; Keith was a real ladies man and he loved to be in the clubs drinking with his boys. I told Pandia that he was the type of man that she'd better keep an eye on, but she said that he loved her and would never leave so I left it alone.

When Pandia told me that she was pregnant I was happy for her and I vowed to be the baby's Godmother. Pandia ended up being put on bed rest early on in her pregnancy, so mom and I took turns playing nurse mate to her while Keith was out working or doing whatever else it was that he did late at night. I'd heard rumors that he was cheating on my sister, but I never told her about it because it was not my place and she was already sick and stressed out from the pregnancy so I felt it best that I dealt with Keith at a later date.

Running into Keith at a club one night was just the opportunity that I needed to confront him about his philandering ways. He had been drinking with his fraternity brothers and fellow St. Louis County police officers from Kappa Psi Kappa so when I walked up to him he didn't know who I was and grabbed my ass.

"How dare you touch me while your wife, my sister lay in bed pregnant with your child!" I yelled over the loud music.

"I didn't know that it was you." He slurred.

"Would it have made it better if I'd been some girl on the street and not

Skeletons

Pandia's sister?"

"I said that I was sorry, damn why do you always have to act like such a bitch towards me."

I reached back to slap his face, but he grabbed my hand and pulled me in to him so close that I could feel the erection beginning to form in his pants, "If I didn't know any better I'd say that you wanted me Asteria."

"If you knew any better you'd let me the fuck go before you wind up missing a few teeth Keith." I spat.

Letting me go he beckoned the bartender, "Let me buy you a drink and let's talk sis."

Rolling my eyes I allowed him to buy me a Grey Goose and Cranberry and we found a spot to talk.

"Why do you hate me Asteria, I haven't done anything to you."

"I don't hate you; I just hate you for my sister."

"But why, I haven't done anything to her."

Rolling my eyes I spat, "Yet. You may have Pandia fooled, Keith, but trust me I know the game and I play it very well."

Keith put his hand on my exposed thigh, "Come on sis, and don't treat me like the enemy when all that I want to be is your friend."

I didn't pull away.

The more we drank, the more we talked and the more I loosened up to Keith. I found him to be funny and very attractive. Before long I was in his arms, he was in my bed, I was on top of him and he was inside of me. Our affair began as one drunken night of lust over three years and one son ago.

Telling Keith that I was pregnant was the hardest thing in my life, he insisted that I get an abortion, but I really wanted a baby so I refused. Keith didn't talk to me the entire pregnancy even when I threatened to tell Pandia who I was pregnant by. He laughed my threat off knowing that I'd never do anything to hurt my sister. It hurt to see my sister and her husband happy over the birth of her son while my own pregnancy was one that I spent alone. Everyone asked me about the whereabouts of Latif's father, but I would lie and tell him that he moved away.

Feeling lonely as I often did when Keith couldn't spend the night with me; I picked up the phone and dialed Jovanna who was still in South Beach.

"Hey what are you doing up so late?" She asked.

Yawning I answered, "Not much, I just couldn't sleep."

"Why, what is the matter?"

"Boy trouble." I pouted.

"Tell me all about it."

Knowing that I could never tell my best friend that I was sleeping with my sister's husband I lied and told her that I was seeing some random guy who could never stay the night with me.

"You need to cut him loose Asteria. If a man can't make time for you then what is the need for him to be in your life? It is obvious to me that he has someone else otherwise he could've spent the night with you. He wasn't trying to run out of there when he was getting his dick wet, was he? Asteria you have got to stop letting this man use you like this." She fussed.

Feeling sorry for myself I said, "You are right Jovanna, but I love him."

"Well that love is one sided."

"He has told me that he loves me too."

"Saying it and showing it are two different things. I'd rather a man never tell me that he loved me, but instead showed me how he felt than a man telling me bullshit just to get what he wants while not showing me shit."

I sighed, "You are right."

"Get it together Asteria; you can do so much better baby." Her tone softened.

"Maybe it is time for me to call it off with him."

"I'm not going to make that decision. You stand alone in this."

"Thanks for the advice, but now I have to get to sleep."

She laughed, "I bet your ass is tired."

"Good bye Jovanna."

"Good night love." She said before hanging up.

I knew that I wouldn't break things off with Keith, I loved him too much and I had too much time invested in him to just end things. Besides Keith promised me that he was going to leave Pandia after Keith Jr. started kindergarten and he and I would move to Seattle, with our son. Until then I'll just have to wait, but at the rate we were going forever seemed like a long time.

9
SANTANA

Standing naked in the hot, steamy bathroom I examined my body as if I were looking at a stranger for the first time. I poured warm almond oil in my hands and ran it along my arms, my breasts and ending at my stomach. I really needed to start joining Jovanna and Justin on their jogs, but I was far too busy for that. I've always had a nice body, but after Mya was born I kept a few of the pounds that I'd gained during my pregnancy. At the age of twenty-four my breasts were still tight and perky; now that I'm thirty-four I can tell the skin starting to lose its tightness. Holding one breast in my hand I squeezed it running the pad of my fingers over my nipple making it hard. Doing the same with my right breast I closed my eyes and ran my tongue across my lips. Pouring more oil in my palms I ran my hands from my ankles, to my calf and up to my full thighs. I spread my thighs apart and ran my hands along the smooth skin of my pussy. I began getting a full bikini wax when Mike and I were still making love three or four times a week, but now that the love-making stopped, waxing was just a habit. I turned on the faucet and sat on the edge of the toilet with my legs spread. Rubbing my clit in a circular motion I bit my bottom lip as not to moan, but the electricity was so intense that I could not help it. With my pointer and middle finger I plunged deep inside of my wetness causing my eyes to roll to the back of my head and my legs to jerk.

"God." I moaned softly hoping the sound of the running water would drown out any noise that might be heard from the other side of the bathroom door.

Deeper and deeper I plunged my fingers inside of my wanting body as the feelings grew more intense and the pressure began to build. Holding on to the side of the sink my body moved with my fingers. My fingers played me like a harp and with every stroke I sang a melody that only I could appreciate until a knock came at the door.

I swallowed hard, "What?"

"Hey I need to get in there." Mike said.

Breathing hard, I slid my fingers out of my body, "I'm just about finished."

"Hurry up, it's getting late."

Rolling my eyes, Mike sure knew how to fuck up a good orgasm.

After I washed my hands I stormed out of the bathroom cutting my eyes at Mike as he lay across the bed with the remote control in his hands.

"What is wrong with you Santana?" he asked as he kept his eyes glued to ESPN.

"Nothing." I shot.

"I know that nothing usually means something in women's terms." He said, "So what is going on?"

"Mike, when was the last time we had sex?" I asked.

"I don't know, last week I guess."

"And are you fine with that?"

He shrugged.

"So you don't care?"

"No, I didn't say that I didn't care, but sex isn't all that important to me anymore."

"Sex is a huge part of a marriage."

"What are you saying Santana; do you want to have sex tonight?" Mike asked never taking his eyes off of Sports Center.

I just looked at him in disbelief.

"If you want to have sex let's do it because I have a very busy day tomorrow, the head honchos are coming in to go over some things and I want to get some sleep tonight." Mike turned the TV off and put the remote down on the bed as he turned toward me.

Turning my back on him I pulled the chocolate duvet back, "Since you have such a busy day tomorrow you'd better get some rest." I said, pissed.

"Why do you have to make this so difficult?" he asked as he kissed the side of my neck, his breath smelled like beer.

"Mike, I'm not in the mood."

Skeletons

"What, but you just said…"

I looked him in his brown eyes and said sternly, "I am not in the mood." Defeated Mike walked into the bathroom slamming the door. I wonder if he was in there finishing up where I began.

We didn't say two words to one another the next morning as we went through our usual morning routine of getting ready for work and getting the kids to school. I watched my husband, the man who at one time could make me come just with one kiss, the man who could at one time make me moan with one touch on my thigh and now he was the man who I no longer felt attracted to. We walked out to our separate cars and waited for one of us to initiate the goodbye kiss.

"Is this about last night?"

I glanced at the silver Donna Karen watch that dangled from my wrist with irritation and leaned forward giving Mike a quick peck on the cheek before turning to my own car leaving him standing in awe.

"Good morning beautiful!" Tabitha chimed as soon as I walked past her desk. She looked even more beautiful than usual in tan pencil skirt that hit her knees and fit her as if the designer made it with her dimensions in mind. The matching jacket hugged her waist and breasts with precision and accuracy and the brown belt that she wore only further accented the fact that Tabitha was a bad bitch.

"Good morning Tabitha." I smiled back suprised at how no matter how bad my day started out seeing Tabitha only made it better.

She handed me a stack of messages, "Mr. Gold called again and wants to meet with you A.S.A.P." She winked.

Rolling my eyes I balled that message up and tossed it in her trash, "he always wants to meet with me A.S.A.P about nothing."

"Hey did you get the invitation to my party that I emailed you yet?"

I looked around the busy office making sure no one heard that question as it is frowned upon for upper management to fraternize with their employees. "No, but I'll check when I get a chance."

My text message alert chimed as soon as I sat in my chair and turned on my computer, it was Mike.

Babe what did I do this time?

I texted back:

Nothing Mike you did absolutely nothing.

Then turned off my cellphone; I really didn't feel like this shit today. After lunch I sat down and opened the email from Tabitha wearing nothing more than a sheer lace bra and panty set with a pair of stilettos, a come hither look in her eyes and a sexy pout on her full red lips.

It was an evite to her twenty-seventh birthday party for that Saturday at The Loft. Smiling at the very seductive picture which was in pure Tabitha fashion, I hovered my mouse over decline just before I clicked the button I looked over at my calendar to see if I had an alibi as to why I couldn't attend her party. Saturday was clear, as usual. Mr. Gold had a strict policy about intermingling with between employees, he said that it causes too many distractions when we should be working and I agreed with him, but I really needed to get out of the house and I was curious to see what it would be like to live one night in Tabitha's world. Reluctantly I hit accept on the evite and closed the picture before I got caught for looking at porn.

As much as I hated to admit it I was looking forward to a night without Mike and the kids, a night for me to have a reason to stay up past midnight and not have to fall asleep while Mike held the remote and watch ESPN until he finally fell asleep.

10
JOVANNA

Exhaling a sigh of relief as we boarded the airplane for our flight back to St. Louis and away from my past. Putting a piece of gum in my mouth and my iPod ear buds in my ears I tried to zone out while listening to Chrissette Michelle, but my mind was not allowing me escape no matter how high up in the sky the airplane climbed my thoughts were still grounded in Memphis.

The memories were still so fresh in my mind that I could almost smell the scent of thick smoke, cheap perfume and stale pussy that burned my nostrils every time I inhaled. That aroma is an odor that I will never forget no matter how much top shelf perfume that I bought. Unlike most of the girls at the Honey Lounge, stepping out on stage was something that I never got used to. Most times I would have to drink three Tom Collins and smoke a blunt before I heard my song being played for me to go out and perform.

With Prince's, Scandalous, thumping through the speakers I would walk on stage after the DJ announced my stage name, Marquita, to the guests. Donning a blonde wig, four and a half inch stilettos that I could barely keep my balance in and a two piece outfit that almost covered my ass; I would slowly strut out onto the stage. As the music played I swayed to the silver pole and touched it softly at first, just I would touch a man, then grabbing the pole I snaked my body around it slowly with the tempo of the music. Closing my eyes I'd imagine that I was not at the Honey Lounge, but that I was dancing for my man, alone in our home while our children slept peacefully in their beds and he watched me lovingly instead of like I was a piece of meat. I had to remove myself from my reality in order to give the men in the club their fantasy.

With my back to the cold metal pole I lifted my arms above my head grabbing the pole as I slid down the length of it parting my legs inches as I slid down the pole. Once in a squatting position I lay on the hardwood floor on my stomach with my back arched with my round ass were in the air and my legs spread, the pole resting in between my ass cheeks. With my eyes closed I could hear the money being dropped on the stage, if I were nothing I was an expert at earning money at the Honey Lounge. Rising up on my knees I unzipped my top exposing the soft flesh of my fresh seventeen-year old breast, making sure to graze each one of them with my fingertips.

Wrapping my left leg around the cold pole I swirled around it getting lost in Prince's voice, his soft whimpers made me moan as I imagined that I was with my lover. Removing the short skirt that covered the barely there thong I wrapped both legs around the pole, leaned back arching my back. For my finale I walked to the edge of the stage, turned around slowly bending at the waist and grabbed my ankles giving the men who were lucky enough to be in the front of the stage a good view. I was not listening to the whistles, cat calls or the men saying what they would do to me later that night as they begged to take me home; I silenced all of that and the only sounds in my ears was the seductive ballad that Prince sang and the soft sounds of money hitting the stage.

Nudging me out of my trance, Tony asked, "Are you alright?"

Smiling I shook my head, closing my eyes, washing my inner turmoil to the tranquil sounds of neo-soul music.

Later that evening as Justin and I lay wrapped in one another's arms my mind was still in limbo. Justin pulled away from me, looking at me with his deep blue eyes he said, "You seem distant today."

Moving hair from my face I said, "I'm fine, I guess that I'm just tired."

"Maybe you should take a break from everything for a while." He suggested.

"I wish that I could Justin, but I have another party coming up."

"I thought that the winter months were your slow season."

"This is slow baby." I kissed him on the tip of his nose.

"I just don't want you to over-work yourself."

"I'm fine; I guess that I'm still a little drained from the party; it got

Skeletons

pretty wild." I got out of bed and walked into the living room to turn up the thermostat, Justin and I were at a never-ending war about the temperature in our house. He liked the house to be at a cool sixty-five degrees where as my people are from Africa and we need the heat so I often cranked the heat up to eighty degrees.

"Leave the thermostat alone Jovanna, it feels good in here." He yelled from the bedroom.

Smiling I walked back into our bedroom, "I don't know what you are talking about Justin."

"Yeah right." He snickered as he turned over on his back.

Kissing him softly on his chest I climbed on top of my soon-to-be husband and wrapped my body around his, "Justin, are there things in your past that you are so ashamed of that you would never tell anyone about?"

Frowning Justin looked at me, "What do you mean?"

"I mean are there things that you have done in your past that you are ashamed of and if anyone found out about you'd be forced to move out of town and change your name." I asked as I toyed with his sandy blonde hair.

"Well, I did impregnate an elderly nun when I was in Catholic school." He joked.

"I'm serious." I said jabbing him in the side.

"To be honest Jovanna, there is nothing in my past that I have to be ashamed of. I have led a normal, stereotypical Caucasian life. What about you; do you have any skeletons in your closet that I should know about?"

I wanted to tell Justin the truth, but I knew that that truth would cost me the man that I loved so I lied, "Not really, my life was pretty boring too."

"I guess that we are just two boring people and that is why I love your boring ass." He whispered as he kissed me on my forehead, "Now get off of me so we can get some sleep."

I felt terrible for not coming clean to Justin, but I couldn't let him know about my past and I would do anything to keep this secret hidden from him.

Shimeka R. McFadden

II
ASTERIA

Fridays were usually our busiest day as clients got their hair done for their weekend activities. While Pandia was styling a client's hair I was in the office looking for new stylist chairs for the booths. Since the salon was doing so well Pandia and I decided to remodel it and I was enjoying shopping for new furniture and fixtures to make Gods and Goddesses one of the best salons around. Hearing a familiar voice I walked out of the office and saw Keith standing at the reception desk kissing Pandia on the cheek.

When Pandia saw me standing there watching them she said, "Asteria, Keith came to take me to lunch, so I'll be back in a few?"

Trying to ignore the fire that was building up in the pit of my stomach I responded, "Are you finished?"

Looking at me sideways Pandia retorted, "I wouldn't be leaving if I weren't, now would I?"

Forcing a smile on my face I walked back to the office making sure I didn't slam the door behind me. How Keith could come down here and take that bitch for lunch? He never took me to lunch, he never takes me anywhere. Grabbing my cell phone off of the desk I sent Keith a text message:

How cute, taking the wife to lunch lol you two are meant for one another.

Keith hated when I talked about his relationship with my sister, but that is all that I could do to keep myself from crying. Instead of sitting in the office feeling sorry for myself I called Santana and Jovanna to meet me for lunch at Pi which was right down the street from the salon.

Santana looked like the professional that she was dressed in a tweed, chocolate, wide-legged business suit with her golden bob hair style softly framing her round face. In college Santana was called freckles because she had a trail of freckles that ran across the bridge of her nose which gave her honey colored skin a youthful appearance. Jovanna, on the other hand, has always been more of the Bohemian type with a pair of wide-legged trouser jeans, a thick chocolate sweater with a black belt and brown cap pulled over her long jet-black hair.

Choosing a booth close to a window we sat down and ordered our drinks, I made sure that I could see out of the window so that I could see Keith and his wife ride by.

"So what is so important that I had to drive all of the way to U-City to eat lunch with you Asteria?" Santana fussed, "You are lucky that I'm not busy today."

I sighed heavily, "Men issues."

"Girl that is the story of our lives." Jovanna said.

"What in the hell are you talking about Jovanna, Justin is too good to you. Hell he has forsaken his own damn family for your black ass where most men can't even forsake their video games for their women.

"No one is perfect; Justin and I have our share of issues too. Don't get it twisted."

"Seriously, Asteria what is going on with you and this unidentified man?" Jovanna asked. "Didn't we just have this conversation the other night?"

"Sometimes I feel as if I'm being played for a fool." I answered.

"If you feel like a nut then you are probably a nut honey." Santana said bluntly as she took a bite of her chicken sandwich.

"There is nothing stronger than the female intuition, listen to your gut." Jovanna said.

If I had listened to my gut I would not be in the situation because my gut told me not to start sleeping with my twin sister's husband in the first place. Now my gut was telling me to walk away, but my heart doesn't want to listen.

"I love this man, yet I feel so empty inside." I said. "When we are together it feels so right, but when he leaves I just want to tear my heart out and throw it out of my window and hit him in the head with it like HERE IT IS TAKE IT!" I exclaimed. "Knowing him, he'd probably just step over it and keep on walking."

Skeletons

"Love is supposed to fill you up not make you feel empty." Jovanna put. "If you are walking away drained then you are not getting what you need."

"After putting in all of the work." Santana added. "You have too many other things going on in your life to let this man dictate your emotions like that. You have the salon and your son to worry about."

Sighing I picked at the salad that the waitress sat in front of me, "But I don't want to be alone. The salon can't hold me at night and my son can't make love to me; I want to be a part of a family."

They listened to me go on and on about the love that I sought from a man that was unavailable to me.

"I feel as if I could spend the rest of my life with him, but then I also feel that I am living in some sort of fantasy land and he is just using me to get what he wants."

"Is this man married?" Santana questioned, "I'm asking because he has all of the signs of a man that is unobtainable."

Catching me off guard with her question, I knocked over a glass of water, spilling it on my jeans, "No, he isn't married, he is just a busy man." My girls looked knowingly at one another, but didn't say another word.

"He seems as if he has some other things going on in his life and that is why he can't fully give you what you need."

"He works a lot." I lied.

"Why haven't we met him yet?" Jovanna asked.

"Because I don't want to keep running men in and out of my friend's lives. When the time is right you all will meet." I lied again, I never intended for Santana and Jovanna to know about Keith and I. They would never understand and it would most likely end our friendship. There are certain rules that as a woman could not be broken, the number one unspoken rule is that you do not sleep with the man of your best friends or sister. While I did sleep with Keith, I never intended to let them in on my secret affair with Keith, instead he and I will move away after he leaves Pandia. I would just have to wait until the time was right and I am more than willing to do so.

"How are you and Mike doing Santana?" I asked changing the subject as a way to divert their prying eyes.

"Married life is just that; married life." She said dryly and bit down into her ham and cheese sandwich leaving a bit of honey Dijon mustard on her lips.

"Wow." Jovanna said, "Is that what I have to look forward to?"

"When Mike and I first got married, he couldn't keep his hands off of me, but now after twelve years of marriage I almost have to beg him for sex."

"You no longer have a sex life?" I asked.

"Unless you call five minutes once or twice a month a sex life." She cut her brown eyes.

"Do you think that he is seeing someone else?" I questioned.

"No, Mike isn't the type that will cheat on me. Honestly I just think that we have just gotten bored with one another."

Jovanna asked, "How do you get bored with your husband? I can't imagine ever getting bored with Justin."

"You have to understand that Mike and I have been together since we were in high school, throughout college and now we have settled into this married life slump. I am a different person than I was in high school and throughout college as is he."

"Are you okay with that?" I asked.

Sighing Santana answered, "I don't know."

"You guys have just lost your spark, there are books, workshops and even retreats that couples can go on in order to ignite that fire that they once had." Jovanna added.

"I don't know if I even want to invest that amount of time into anything like that." She sighed. "Besides Mike believes the only help that we need is the help of prayer and God."

"That is a Preacher's son for you." Asteria smiled.

Looking at her in disbelief I said, "Marriage is an investment Santana, and like any other investment you have to invest in it. You and Mike have been together since high school that is a long time to just throw away. Lasting marriages are so rare these days, I just don't want to see your marriage fail."

"Who said that we were failing?" Santana shot, "All I said that was we have fallen into a slump and this is common for couples who have been together for some time. Don't worry we will be alright."

"What are you ladies up to for the weekend?" I asked changing the subject as it was clear that Santana didn't want to talk about her marriage any further.

"I have a full plate dealing with wedding stuff and I have that to meet with a client to go over her party plans." Jovanna said, "I'm going to be pretty busy."

"As usual." I said, "You never sit still."

"Well, I was invited to a party." Santana announced with excitement.

With a raised eyebrow I asked, "Who invited you to a party?"

"My assistant, Tabitha." She answered. "Damn have I gotten so lame that it is impossible for me to be invited to parties?" Santana laughed.

"Isn't she the dark skinned girl with the long extensions?" Jovanna asked.

Skeletons

"Yes, she is a great assistant."
"She is a brick house." Jovanna exclaimed, "She is a cute girl, thank God you are a female and not one of those horny men or else she would have a hard time getting her work done."
"Remember our twenties?" I asked.
We all laughed.
Santana spoke, "I remember them and I'm so glad that they are over. I love my thirties; I know who I am, and where I want to be."
I agreed, "Your twenties are all about exploration, but they are filled with so many uncertainties and insecurities."
"If I could have my twenty-something body with my thirty-something mind I would be one bad bitch!" Jovanna joked.
We laughed so loud that people were looking our way and that is how it was when I got together with my two best friends; they always made me feel better no matter how large the storm cloud was that chased me.
When I got back to the salon, Pandia was styling a client; whatever she and Keith did on her lunch break must've been good because she was wearing a smile from ear to ear. She could smile all that she wanted, because he would be at my house tonight and by tomorrow that stupid smile would be replaced by tears.

Shimeka R. McFadden

12
SANTANA

The sounds of hip hop rang through my ears as I made my way through The Loft for Tabitha's birthday party. I had second thoughts about coming, but after the argument that Mike and I got into I quickly changed my mind and couldn't wait to get out of the house. I managed to squeeze my way through the crowd and find a seat at the bar next to a model thin woman in an electric blue jumpsuit with micro-braids that reached the middle her her exposed back.

She ran her dark eyes all over my body and smirked at my decision to wear a Diane Vonfurstenberg dress and boots. I was dressed more for a dinner meeting than a club.

"Hi, I'm Lashonda" she introduced. "Good luck getting a drink."

"Hello Lashonda, I'm Santana." I smiled.

"I love your dress; where did you get it from?" She asked

"I don't remember I've had this for a while."

She smiled as if she knew that I'd pulled the vintage dress out of the back of my closet.

Tabitha would often tell me about different people that she met, but I wouldn't have imagined that her birthday party would have been so packed. It was practically standing room only in the VIP section of the club.

"How do you know Tab?" She asked.

"I work with her."

"That is how we met too." she half-smiled as her eyes danced arouond my body a second time.

Uncomfortable with the way her almond-shaped eyes roamed my body I began watching the crowd.

"Is it usually this busy here?"

Lashonda laughed, "You don't get out much do you Santana?"

"How could you tell?" I smiled.

"It is always this busy in any club in this city. It seems that there is nothing else to do besides go to work Monday through Friday, go to the club on Saturday then go to church on Sunday."

"Are you from around here?"

She shook her head, "No I'm from L.A. I only flew to St. Louis because Tab insisted that I come to her birthday party."

"You are here for one night?"

"Yes and I can't wait to leave." She tossed her braids over her shoulder.

"You and Tabitha must be good friends for you to have flew all of the way up here just to celebrate her bithday."

Winking at me, she whistled loudly catching the bartender's attention "Hey can we get some service?" she yelled.

The bartender finished his last order and made his way towards us.

I raised an eyebrow, impressed with how bold she was.

I ordered a glass of Moscato and she ordered a long island ice tea which she quickly guzzled half-way down.

"That hit the spot." She smiled. "Now I'm ready to dance! Do you want to join me?"

"No thanks, I think that I'm going to park it right here for a while."

"I know that you didn't come to this club just to sit at the bar Santana, come on dance with me I promise that I don't bite." she winked her long eyelashes.

I laughed, "Maybe later."

"I am going to hold you to that sexy." She said before walking on to the dance floor.

As I watched Lashonda walk through the crowd I noticed Tabitha in the corner having what seemed like a heated conversation with an older woman who seemed out of place in the club. Wearing a black blazer over a crisp white shirt, khaki pants and black flats the salt and pepper haired woman seemed angry at Tabitha. I watched as Tabitha turned to walk away only for the woman to grab Tabitha by the arm. Yanking away

Skeletons

Tabitha pointed a finger in the woman's face, snaked her neck as she said a few words then walked away, leaving the woman standing with tears in her eyes. Noticing that I was watching the exchange Tabitha walked my way.

She looked stunning in a fire engine red corset that barely contained her double D breast; the pair of skinny jeans that looked airbrushed on her curvacous body and a pair of stiletto Louboutin peep-toed heels that gave her short stature four additional inches.

"Santana, I'm glad that you made it!" her embrace took me by surprise.

"Is everything okay?" I asked with a concerned look on my face.

"I'm cool; are you having fun?" she smiled.

"Yes, you have a nice turn out. Unfortunately I have to leave, I have to get home to the family." I said.

"No don't leave!" she pouted, "The party is just getting started."

"It's getting late and I have to go to church in the morning."

"Church?" she mused, "I never would have thought of you to be a Bible thumping Christian woman Santana."

I laughed, "I'm not a Bible thumping Christian woman; my husband's parents are the Pastor and First Lady of the church so I'm kind of obligated to go."

"Oh so you married the son of a Preacher man," she giggled, "How sexy."

"If that is what you want to call it." I said seemingly less than enthused.

"Come on live a little and do a shot with me before you go." She grabbed my hand and led me back to the bar. Looking back I saw the look of scorned written on the face of the woman who Tabitha had words with. Ignoring my protests, Tabitha proceeded to order two shots of Patron. Holding up her glass to mine she winked and said, "Happy birthday to me!" and threw the warm, bitter tasting liquor to the back of her throat swallowing hard.

"Come on dance with me." She urged, "It's my birthday."

Of all of the men in the room, it was shocking that she wanted me to dance with her. As Tabitha ignored my many protest leading me to the dance floor by my hand, we stepped onto the crowded dance floor; when I looked back the woman scorned was gone.

"You need to loosen up a bit." She said, "You act like you are an old lady."

"That is what I feel like sometimes." I yelled over the quick tempo of Lil Wayne.

"You are far too attractive to feel like that." Tabitha winked as she dropped to the floor, making her body snake as she came back up; she was so close to me that I could smell her Perry Ellis perfume. "The son of a Preacher man is a very lucky man." She breathed as she gyrated on my body; I watched the sweat run from the back of her neck down her bare back to no man's land.

I swallowed hard trying to ignore that familiar feeling that I hadn't felt in a long time, "Tell him that."

"Maybe I will or maybe it will be our little secret." Tabitha ran the tips of her fingers along my already sweaty face, "It's getting hot in here."

Confused by her last gesture I continued to dance with her, Tabitha was too close for comfort, but I didn't want her to go. I tried to ignore the fact that I enjoyed the uncomfortable coziness that Tabitha's hot, sweaty body offered as we swayed together to the sounds of the music. I don't know if it was the Patron, but for a moment it felt as if my dance partner and I were the only two people in the room. Feeling the softness of her hand on my thigh as she pulled me closer made me want to hold it there forever. Confused and soaked with the smell of our sweat mixed with that of our perfumes, I walked off of the dance floor leaving Tabitha behind.

Making my way into the bathroom I tried to regain my composure, wiping sweat from my forehead and neck. Soon Tabitha was standing beside me with another drink in her hand.

"Tabitha I really have to go." I protested, but she handed me the drink and smiled.

"Santana, you are a gorgeous woman, but sometimes I feel as if you underestimate yourself. Have you gotten so use to being a wife and a mother that you have forgotten how to be a woman and a lover?"

Shocked by her audacious question I asked, "What do you mean?"

"I mean, I don't think that Mike is doing his job." She put bluntly.

Exposed by what Tabitha said I downed the drink. Tabitha said, "Sexually."

"Tabitha, I assure you, Mike and I are doing fine."

"Please, is that why your eyes roll whenever he calls or texts you? Is that why you always come to work in a huff? Is that why you look so horny right now, that you could fuck anyone in the other room like a dog in heat?" She whispered in my ear. "You want something Santana, but you won't allow yourself to fuel the fire that is slowly dying inside of you."

"I'm not like that Tabitha, Mike and I just hit a bump, but it will get better."

"When will it get better? When Mike finally decides to pay attention to you? Why does Mike get to decide when it will get better? You need to take matters into your own hands and take care of yourself."

"I do take care of myself." I said my head spinning.

I felt Tabitha's hand on my upper thigh as she whispered in my ear, "Baby, finger fucking yourself three times a week is not taking care of you."

I stood silently, trying to swallow whatever I was feeling in the pit of my stomach.

"Here," she said handing me a tiny blue pill that was in the shape of a Smurf, "Take this and really take care of yourself." Tabitha popped a pill in her mouth.

"What is this?" I asked looking at the pill.

"This is your escape; this is your turn to take care of yourself for a chance." She was so close to me that her breasts were on my arm and her lips were grazing my neck, "Just open your mouth and put it in it is not that difficult." She whispered seductively.

Tabitha had me in a trance as I did exactly what she told me to do.

"Now sit back and enjoy the ride." She whispered.

Hearing the music in my ears was one thing, but now I could feel it in my body, coursing through my veins, my heart beating in sync with the music. Tabitha was no longer with me; she was back on the dance floor. I watched her move as if she and I were the only ones in the room with the music playing tunes that only we understood. As if in some sort of spell, I walked onto the dance floor and began dancing with Tabitha.

We moved together as if we had fire inside of our bodies and needed one another to put it out. Tabitha snaked her body against mine like she was a pro, grinding her soft ass against my body and me grabbing her hips pulling her towards me. My hands wanted to touch Tabitha's soft, moist skin; my lips wanting to suck hers as we moved to the beat of the music. I felt as if I were a King Cobra in a trance and my snake charmer was dancing in front of me and I never wanted to stop.

13
JOVANNA

It was after two in the morning when I felt Justin get up from the bed and walk into the living room to answer the phone.
"Who was that baby?" I yawned when he got back into bed.
"They had the wrong number." He mumbled.
Pulling the duvet back over my shoulder I asked, "Who did they ask for?"
"He asked for Marquita; let's get back to sleep."
My once drowsy eyes were wide open with my heart was pounding. Wide awake I got out of bed.
"Where are you going?" Justin asked.
"It's freezing in here; I'm going to turn up the heat." I fibbed as I shuffled out of the bedroom and into the living room. I grabbed the cordless phone and took it into the living room so that Justin wouldn't hear me looking through the caller ID; I scrolled the last number dialed and to my amazement they hadn't called anonymous, but from a St. Louis area code. Knowing that I couldn't call the number right back, I wrote it on a post it note and slid it in my nightstand drawer.
"I hope you didn't turn the heat up on hell Jovanna, you know that I get hot." Justin nagged.
Disregarding him I tried to get some sleep before I called that number back in the morning.

Closing my eyes, I could see his face just as if he were standing in front of me; his face was a face that I could never forget.

Dancing at the club was something that I hated, but it afforded me a nice room that I rented, it put food in my once hungry stomach and the ability to keep my hair and nails done.

Stripping for money started taking a toll on my mind. I no longer cared about men; in my eyes they were all lousy hounds who came to the club to escape their responsibilities at home. The way that they drooled over the dancers when we put our ass in their faces, was pathetic. How dumb of a woman to allow her man to come home smelling of alcohol and another woman's pussy.

I was finishing a dance to Prince's 'Do Me Baby' with my legs spread and my pussy in some woman's husband's face as he flicked his rent money on top of me; when the song was over and I collected my money I looked to my left and there he was dressed in a red three piece suit with matching gators and fedora. His gold cuff links were the only sparkle in the dimly lit club while the smoke from the thick cigar perched between his lips billowed over his face.

With the snap of his perfectly manicured fingers Chad could have had any girl in the Honey Lounge. We all knew who he was and what he was about because most of us wanted to be a part of it. Chad and his crew hardly ever stepped into the strip club unless it was in search of a new girl. I was mesmerized by his blue-black skin, dark curly hair and eyes as light as honey. The thick scar that ran from the left side of his neck to the right intrigued yet repulsed me. No one knew how he'd gotten the war wound, but I heard that the other guy didn't walk away from that fight.

Chad was one of the most well-known pimps in Memphis, everyone knew that to mess with him or his girls and his girls knew not to mess with his money. Part of his game was knowing the right things to say in order to get inside of a girls head; once he got inside of her head, he made her worship him by telling her about all of the money that he had, how powerful that he was and how she could be a big part of his world instead of a small part in her own and that was it, she was forever his; the younger the better. Chad didn't deal with girls over the age of twenty-five, he preferred his girls young, because the older the girl the harder it she was to control. He picked girls who had nothing to run to, girls who were running from something and girls who didn't have anyone coming to look for them.

I was a seventeen-year-old who thought that I knew it all, but Chad erased all that I thought that I knew and replaced it with what he

Skeletons

wanted me to know in return I became who he wanted me to be. He was my puppet master, when Chad pulled a string I did exactly as he commanded.

Chad got me away from the Honey Lounge and into his apartment where he manipulated me into doing whatever it was that he wanted me to do. I was hated among the other girls because he chose me to be his "girlfriend", but in this profession, a Queens's reign is short-lived. Always trying to keep his love and interest, I made sure I did everything that he wanted. That included selling my body to strangers in cars, alleys and shitty hotels.

I was one of six girls that Chad had working for him, and each one of us had a quota of at least three-hundred dollars a night and if we didn't make his money we better stay out on the block until we did and he didn't care if our feet bled, we'd better not call him for a ride or we'd be riding home in the trunk of his Cadillac. If any girl came up short, he made sure she knew better than to come up short again. Being one of Chad's girls was not about the money because we never saw any of it once it went into Chad's pocket; it was about the status.

The next morning after Justin left for work, I went into the living room and dialed the number with my heart pounding in my chest.

"Marquita, I knew that you would call." The deep familiar voice with the thick Southern drawl said after the fifth ring. I could hear him take a drag out of the Don Diego cigar.

"Don't call me that."

"Have you become so high and mighty that you forgot where you came from?" He laughed.

"What do you want?"

"You know what I want; you took it from me years ago."

"I only took what was mine Chad." I said as I paced the room biting my nails as I often did when I was nervous.

He laughed deeply, "Yours? Bitch I made you!" he yelled into the phone. His yell made me jump almost dropping the phone, "I made you and don't you ever forget that. If it weren't for me you would still be dancing for dollars at the Honey Lounge!"

I wanted to know how he got my number, but I already knew who told him and why. Tasha was Chad's favorite girl before I came around and she was always jealous of the relationship that he and I had. She sold me out, she told him about my business and where I was based out of after running into her at the party. I knew that she could not be trusted, but what I didn't know was why she was still dealing with Chad when she had a great career.

I could hear Chad take another puff of the cigar; I could remember the strong smell of those Cuban cigars that he smoke and it made me want to vomit and I also remembered the large marks they'd leave after he burnt me on the leg with one.

"Who was that who answered the phone last night Marquita? Tell me does he know who you really are? Does he know how much money you made on the corner of Fifth and Washington?"

"Don't worry about who that was who answered my phone. What do you want?"

"Don't play dumb with me hoe, I want what is due to me, I want my damn money!" he yelled then regained his composure, "You are lucky that I have let it go this long, but I'm trying to give you the benefit of doubt. I want you to doubt yourself the next time you fuck with a man like me. I want you to doubt your intelligence the next time the thought crosses your mind to steal money from a man like me."

"Fuck you!" I screamed, "You owed me that money, you stole so much more from me than I ever took from you!"

"We had a deal Marquita; didn't your momma ever warn you about making deals with the devil?"

"You made me a scared, little girl and you wanted me to stay that way and now you are mad that I finally left."

"Don't kid yourself hoe, you were just one of many and easily replaced."

"Like I said before, fuck you and don't you ever call this phone again!"

14
ASTERIA

With my arms folded across my chest as I stood in the doorway to my apartment refusing to let Keith inside.
"Are you going to let me in?" he smiled.
"Why should I?" I protested not moving an inch.
Keith moved closer to me, the sexy scent of his cologne made me want to hold him close, "Because you know that you want some of this."
"I'm sorry I don't do sloppy seconds."
"You've been doing seconds for a few years, so what has changed?"
"Why did you take her out to lunch today Keith, do you realize how I felt?"
"Well it's not like you don't know that I'm married Asteria." He said.
I rolled my eyes, "You never take me to lunch?"
Keith kissed me softly on the cheek, "I will do better I promise. Come on, it's cold out here." He said pushing past me and into my home.
"She gets lunch and I get late night dick; hardly seems fair Keith." I said as I watched him play with our son. There are many nights when Keith came over and we ate dinner then took care of Latif together I imagined this as our life only to awaken to the harsh reality that my son and I are always on borrowed time.

"I'm getting tired of living this way Keith."

Sighing heavily Keith looked at me with agitation in his eyes, "Asteria, I really don't feel like this. Every time I come over here lately we have to have this same conversation."

"You are damn right we have the same conversation because I feel like you are using me!" I fussed.

"Asteria, don't yell in front of my son." He warned.

"No, your son is little Keith; Latif is only your son between the hours of 9 PM to whenever you feel like leaving. Admit it Keith, we come second!"

Keith picked up Latif and took him upstairs to his bedroom, soon I could hear Keith giving him a bath and putting him to bed as I cleaned up the kitchen and living room. Keith came downstairs and pulled me close to him, but I pushed away in defiance.

"Not tonight Keith, I'm not in the mood."

"What is your problem girl?"

I didn't answer him.

"What more do you want from me Asteria? You went into this with your eyes wide open; I never forced you to start fucking me and you know this. You have been acting like a little kid lately with all of this pouting and carrying on. I don't have time for this shit."

"Don't tell me what you don't have time for Keith!" I yelled, "I don't have time for your constant bullshit."

"What constant bullshit?"

"You telling me that you are going to leave Pandia and we are moving to Seattle to be together as a fucking family." I muffed him in his forehead and walked away.

Keith put his head down in his hands, "Asteria how many times do I have to tell you that it is not as cut and dry as you think."

"You go home tell her you no longer love her, pack up and leave; how hard is that Keith?"

"That is my fucking wife!" he yelled trying to keep his composure, "She is your fucking sister! Don't you have any heart?"

"Really how soon I forget with the way you run up in here all hours of the night!"

"So what are you saying Asteria?" Keith said.

"Leave her." I demanded.

"In time." He stood his ground.

"You can't come around here any longer until you leave her."

Keith looked at me in disbelief, "That is your sister Asteria."

"She knows that you are fucking someone else Keith; she is not stupid. I get tired of hearing her cry about how you didn't come home this night or how you smelled like pussy the next and then see you come take her to lunch in my face like I'm not shit!"

"That is my wife."

"You said that you loved me."

Keith took my hand, "I do love you, but I just can't leave Pandia like that." No matter how I tried to fight it, a single tear rolled down my face Keith stood and wiped it away and kissed me. "I do love you, but just give me some time."

"I'm tired of waiting."

Keith began kissing me on my neck, the softness of his lips made me weaken, "Me too." Taking my hand Keith led me to the leather sectional sitting me down.

He kissed my fingertips, taking my ring finger into his wet mouth while looking deeply into my eyes. He knew how to get what he wanted out of me. Unzipping his brown uniform pants and pulling out his long, thick dick Keith took my hand and wrapped it around his shaft.

"Show me how much you love this." He moaned Keith loved to have his dick touched and sucked.

Smiling up at my dark stallion I licked my lips before playfully licking the head of his dick making it grow even harder.

"I love your lips baby." He moaned.

Kissing his dick softly I said, "Do you love that daddy?"

"Damn baby I do, I do, I do." He moaned loudly.

Taking my tongue I ran it up and down the length of his dick using my lips to suck the sides of it as my right hand squeezed it and my left hand cupped his balls giving them soft embraces. Keith's body jerked as I wrapped my soft lips around his dick and work my mouth magic on him as my hands went to work on his shaft and balls. Keith's moans grew louder and louder as he gripped my hair with both hands.

"Damn. Baby. This. Shit. Feels. So. Fucking. Good." Keith stammered as I tried to suck love from his dick, "Deep throat that dick baby."

I threw my head back and took the entire length of his dick inside of my mouth, swallowing as I tried to keep myself from gagging.

"I am about to cum!" he growled.

Trying to pull him out of my mouth, Keith gripped the back of my head as he released his seeds which filled my mouth with the thick, warm fluid.

"Show me that you love me and swallow that shit." He moaned as he came in my mouth.

Wiping my mouth Keith said, "Your sister never lets me come in her mouth and that is why I love you."

Shimeka R. McFadden

I proved my love to him that night, but the true humiliation came after brushing my teeth, I walked downstairs to find Keith gone as if he were never there. He didn't even say goodbye.

15
SANTANA

Mike wore a satisfied smile Sunday when I came down for breakfast. He and the kids were already dressed for church.
"Did you enjoy your night?" he asked giving me a wink.
"I haven't danced like that since college." I said pouring myself a glass of orange juice. "My legs are sore."
Mike smacked me on my butt, "Your legs don't hurt from dancing all night." He winked, "I was going to the gym, but you gave me quite the work out last night."
Trying to remember what exactly happened, I sat at the breakfast bar. I remembered taking the blue pill and dancing with Tabitha as if we were lovers. I recalled driving home in a daze, parking my van in the driveway and coming into the house to find Mike fast asleep in bed. Stripping down to nothing, I climbed on top of my husband surprising him, but not caring. I kissed him on the mouth with the passion that I had for him when we were in high school; my hands roaming on familiar territory as if I'd never traveled there before. Feeling Mike harden through his lounge pants I pulled them down and rode him as if he were a Bronco and I was trying to win the Lane Frost award. Mike called my name so loudly that I was sure he would wake the kids, but at that point I didn't care.

"Did you hear me?" He asked bringing me back to reality.

"I'm sorry, what did you say?"

"Are you going to make it to service this morning?"

"Not today Mike, I'm tired. You and the kids can go without me; I need to rest before work tomorrow."

With the look of disappointment in his eyes Mike said, "Dad will be disappointed not to see you there, but I understand. Go ahead and get you some rest and we will see you this afternoon." Mike kissed me on the cheek then he and the kids left for church.

Climbing back into bed I checked my cell phone, I had one text message from Tabitha that read:

You really know how to get loose! Hope you had as much fun as I did. C U Monday.

Smiling I rolled over in bed and went back to sleep. It felt good to have the house to myself and not have to get dressed up only to sit in church for hours and pretend to be happy.

The following day while I was at work, Tabitha knocked on my door with a bright smile on her face.

"Good morning sunshine!" she smiled brightly.

Returning her smile I said, "Good morning to you too."

"Did you have fun Saturday night?" she whispered.

"I did, but I have a question."

"Hopefully I have an answer." She leaned against my desk; her exotic floral scent filled my space. My eyes roamed to her abundant thighs as I tried to fight the feeling that was churning in the pit of my stomach. Clearing my throat I asked, "What was that pill that you gave me?"

Raising an arched eyebrow Tabitha asked, "Did you like that?"

"I'm not saying all of that," I laughed, "But what was it?"

"Freedom is what I like to call it, but some call it harmony."

"I did feel free and harmonious."

"Did you feel the music coursing through your body and that you could dance all night?"

"I felt like I could fly."

Throwing her head back Tabitha laughed, "Gosh, I love feeling like that."

"I went home and actually had sex with my husband!" I exclaimed.

We both laughed.

"I'm jealous." She winked, "Would you like to feel like that again?"

Thinking I answered, "I want to feel like that every day."

"The ultimate escape." She moaned.

"And I want to escape every fucking day." I whispered while looking into her eyes.

Just then a knock was at my door, it was June from Payroll, "I'm sorry Mrs. Montgomery, but I needed to speak with you about some discrepancies with the payroll."

Tabitha stood up and straightened her red pencil skirt, tossing her hair over her shoulder, "Okay I will have those aging reports on your desk by noon." She winked, "Good morning June, love that sweater."

I couldn't help but let my eyes wander towards Tabitha's ass as she switched out of my office.

I tried hard to listen to June talk about the payroll not adding up but I couldn't concentrate with Tabitha's exotic scent still in the air. I don't know what it is about her, but every time I was around her I felt more alive than what I have ever felt. Maybe it was the fact that she was so young and carefree while I was in my thirties and had so many responsibilities or maybe it was me reliving my college experiments all over again.

16
JOVANNA

Justin and I met at The Boathouse in Forest Park in order to speak with the caterer about our upcoming rehearsal dinner. As the caterer talked my focus was on the conversation that I had with Chad Sunday morning.

"Hey are you alright Jovanna?" Keith asked as we looked over the menu.

"Yes, I'm fine." I faked a smile.

"You seem off in your own today."

"I'm sorry; I'm just a little tired." I lied, "What do you think about the menu choices?"

Justin looked at me in disbelief for a moment, but turned his attention back to the menu, "Honey, I really don't care what they serve at the reception." Looking at me he added, "Jovanna, I really hope you are being honest and that you are not hiding anything from me."

Swallowing hard, I touched Justin on the side of his face, smiling softly I reassured him, "Baby everything is fine." I kissed his thin, pink lips.

"Aww, look at the two love birds." The caterer smiled as she walked back into the room to see if we made our choices.

After finalizing things with the caterer Justin had to get back to work. Before getting into our cars he pulled me close to him wrapping his arms around my body in a tight bear hug. The warmth of his strong body made me forget about the cold air that whipped around us.

"You make me happy Jovanna, and I hope that I make you feel the same way. If you are having second thoughts about this please just let me down easily and don't leave me standing at the alter looking like a dick." Suddenly I had a strange feeling in the pit of my stomach; it felt as though we were being watched. I looked to my left then to my right and didn't see anything out of the ordinary, but my face carried a worried looked. "I love you too Justin and baby don't worry I wouldn't even think of leaving you." I managed through the thick lump in my throat. Kissing him on his cheek I pulled away, "You'd better get back to work baby."

"Are you sure that everything is alright with you?"

I sighed heavily and pulled my car keys out of my coat pocket, "Justin, I told you that I'm fine."

"I know I just hate to think that we are going to enter our marriage with secrets between us. I don't think that I could live with that."

Looking into his eyes I said, "Who is keeping secrets?"

"I feel that there is this brick wall in between us and while you will let me peek over it you won't let me on the other side."

"Babe, there are no secrets could you please stop asking me that?" Changing the subject I asked, "Have you talked to your mom about me taking her and your aunt to get their dresses for the wedding."

When Justin didn't answer I knew that he hadn't. "Well at least now we know who has been keeping the secrets." I retorted letting his hand go and getting into my car.

On my way back home I dialed Asteria's cellular phone and she picked up on the first ring as if she were expecting a call.

"Hey sugar." She sang.

"Are you busy?" I asked "I need a touch up."

"Come on over I can squeeze you in with Londyn. Is everything alright?" she asked.

"Yes, I'm fine. I was at the Boathouse with Justin and since I am still in the area I decided to stop by to get a touch up because my roots are nappy as hell." I explained as I looked at my hair in the rearview mirror.

"Just come right in; Londyn had a cancelation so you should be able to get right in."

As soon as I stepped into the stylish salon, Aaron started singing Stevie Wonder's song, Jungle Fever. Flipping him the middle finger I walked over and hugged him, "Why do you always have to sing that dumb ass song whenever I see you Aaron."

"It is all with love." He kissed me on the cheek, "How have you been I haven't seen you in months?"

Skeletons

"I've been great, just busy planning." I smiled

"I am not mad at you at all." He said as he rolled his clients long locks between his hands.

"Hey Londyn." I waved to her while she finished the client before me. "Hi Keisha." I smirked.

Pandia walked out of the back room and hugged me, "You look good!" she squealed.

"You too, girl your dropped all of that baby weight."

Pandia smacked my hand, "Heifer you know that little Keith is four!"

Asteria was sitting at the front desk and I noticed how she rolled her eyes when Pandia mentioned her son, "Hey girl what's up?" I asked.

Smacking her red lip gloss she answered, "Not shit at all girl, just going through these bills." she held up a stack of mail and dropped it on the desk.

Adjusting my green purse on my arm I asked, "Why are you acting like you have an attitude today?"

"I don't have an attitude; I am just a little tired."

"Well, can I talk to you privately for a moment?" I asked.

Asteria looked crazy at Pandia and said, "Hey, I'm going to the back room to talk to Jovanna for a minute. Do you think that you can hold things down?"

Looking at the clock that hung on the back wall Pandia answered, "Yes, I can hold it down Asteria; just be sure that you are back soon because Keith is picking me up so that we can meet with the party planner at Monkey Joes for little Keith's birthday party."

"Oh, his birthday is coming up isn't it?" Asteria said as if she didn't know when her only nephew's birthday was. "Wow, make sure you remind me when it is so that I can bring Latif."

Pandia rolled her eyes at her sister while she finished up her client.

"What was that all about girl?" I asked.

Asteria picked up her cell phone and began texting as if she were upset by something.

"Asteria, what's up girl?" I asked, but she ignored me as she finished her text.

Slamming her phone down on the desk she ran her fingers through her sandy hair, "Niggas girl!" she fumed, "I'm sorry, but what's going on with you?"

"I just left the Boathouse with Keith" I began

"For the reception dinner right?" she smiled, "How did it go?"

"It went alright, but…"

"But, come on Jovanna, you know that I can't stand a but in a sentence!"

she fussed, "But what?"

I sighed, "I feel as if Justin really doesn't know me as well as he thinks he does and I don't want him getting hurt."

Asteria looked at me with widened eyes, "What in the hell are you talking about Jovanna? You are one of the best women that I know."

Standing I began to pace the room, "How do you know that?"

"Because I have known you for over ten years and I have never known for you to be anything but a good woman. Why are you tripping today girl?"

I needed to tell her who I really am, "Asteria there is something that I need to tell you, but I need you to listen and keep an open mind."

"I'm all ears." She said, but just when I was about to tell her about my past her cell phone vibrated on the desk. Asteria held up one well-manicured finger and answered the phone call.

"Hello. What do you mean I'm tripping? Hold on" she put the phone to her side and looked at me, "Hey Jovanna can we finish this conversation in a few, I have to take this?"

Smiling I grabbed my purse and walked out of the office; just as I rounded the corner Londyn beckoned me to her chair. I was ready for a change, I told Londyn not only to touch up my roots, but also to cut my neck-length hair into a short pixie style like Nia Long wore her hair. Despite the protests of Londyn, Aaron and Pandia I demanded that my stylist chop it all off and give me a new beginning. Watching in the mirror I knew that changing my look on the outside wouldn't change who I was on the inside.

17
ASTERIA

Putting the phone back up to my ear I spat, "I hope Latif's next party gets to be thrown at Monkey Joe's." I spat.

Keith sighed into the phone, "Let's not start this again Asteria."

Rolling my eyes I said, "Where are you?"

"I just turned onto Delmar and I'll be there in five minutes to pick up Pandia."

"Keith, I'm getting tired of playing second fiddle to my sister. All of my life no matter how much I accomplished I was still second compared to her. Do you realize how much it hurts me to see you and her together while I'm all alone?"

"Yes I do realize that Asteria but I hate to sound harsh when I say these are the breaks when you fuck around with a married man."

"I kick myself for it every day, but I can't help the way that I feel about you."

"How do you feel about me?" he said taunting me.

I smiled, "Don't play Keith you already know how much I love you."

"I love it when you say that, but I love it even more when you moan it."

"Would you like for me to moan it for you tonight, baby?" I asked seductively.

"Damn you keep a nigga's dick rock hard don't you? But I can't stop through tonight."

"Why not, did you promise your wife that you'd be a good boy and keep your ass at home for a change?"

"No, actually I'm going out with Stony and Pete for a guy's night out."

"Fine, I guess I will have to wait until tomorrow night then."

"Maybe, but I have to go because I just pulled up to your shop."

After hanging up with Keith, I logged into the internet and paid a few bills and ordered the stylists new smocks; I couldn't bear to see Keith pick up my sister again. When I thought that it was safe, I walked out of the office and into the main salon where I saw Jovanna sitting under the dryer and Keith was sitting in Keisha's chair while she gave him a lining.

"What's up Asteria?" Keith spoke when he saw me. "How is Latif?"

Wanting to cut my eyes at him, I answered, "Latif is doing fine; too bad his no good daddy doesn't get to see him often or he'd see how big he has gotten."

Keith's jaw tightened, "That is too bad, but you have to do what you have to do. Maybe next time you will find you a man that is willing to marry you before you have his baby."

That was low. "Maybe I will Keith, maybe I will."

"Asteria, after I finish Mya I'm heading out for the rest of the day." Pandia said.

Since she was almost finished with her last client there was no issue with her leaving early. "That is cool, girl. What's going on with you and Keith tonight?"

"Nothing much, he is going out with the guys and I'm staying home, but it won't make any sense for me to drive all of the way out on Watson Road to Monkey Joe's then try to make it back here when I don't have anymore clients."

"You are right, have fun." I smiled, "I'm going back in the office, and I have paperwork to get started on."

Looking at Keith flirt with Keisha made my blood boil, "Keith, it was nice seeing you again."

"You too; take care." He said without taking his eyes off of Keisha.

Later that night after putting Latif to bed I sent Keith a text:

Hey baby, why don't you ditch the boys and come over I've got something that I want you to see.

After waiting fifteen minutes and no response I laid across the bed, spread my legs and took a picture of my freshly shaven pussy and sent it to Keith. After waiting another ten minutes and no response I decided to do some investigating to figure out where he was.

"Hello?" Pandia answered the phone.

Skeletons

"Hey girl what are you doing?"

"Nothing, just sitting here watching television; I just put little Keith to bed." She yawned.

"It sounds like you are waiting for Keith to get home." I joked.

"Girl please, I'd be waiting up all night if that were the case." She said, "You know how he is. He didn't come home until the sun came up last night."

He was not with me, fuming I asked, "Where is he at now?"

"He said that he was going to the Skybox with his boys."

"Do you believe him?"

"Yes, I just called him and text Stony's wife and she confirmed that he is at the Skybox and Keith is with him."

"That is good; at least you know that he is not knee deep in some pussy."

"For now that is, I am so sick of this to be honest with you; some days I just want to give up, leave him and move out of town." She sighed, "And do you want to know what? I doubt that he would even miss us."

I did not know what to say to her, on one hand I wanted to tell my sister that I would take her to the divorce lawyer in the morning and buy her a plane ticket in the afternoon, but on the other hand it really hurt me to know that Keith was treating her this way.

"You just have to do what is best for you and your piece of mind Pandia; you can't keep pleasing someone else while you are unhappy."

"I understand what you are saying; I have to learn to put myself first. I don't see how you did it."

"Did what?" I asked.

"How you just let go of Latif's dad like you did and chose to raise your son by yourself. I wish that I was as strong as you are, Asteria; I've always admired your strength."

I wanted to tell her that I haven't let my son's father go, I wanted to tell her that I was about to go out and find her husband, my son's father and bring him home with me tonight, but instead I said, "I don't know how I do it sometimes either, but I guess I got my strength from mom."

My twin laughed, "Yeah mom was the epitome of strength with all of the shit that she put up with from daddy."

"Love makes you do some crazy things." I smiled thinking of our late mother.

Pandia yawned again, "Well I'm about to go to sleep, I can't wait up on him all night tonight."

"Alright, I will see you in the morning."

"Asteria, I love you."

Taken by surprise I stammered, "I-I love you too."

Shimeka R. McFadden

Once I hung up the phone with her I jumped out of bed, threw on a pair of jeans, a hoodie, and boots. I got Latif out of his bed and put his coat on over his thermal sleeper as he slept. Jumping in my blue Avalon I sped down the road towards the highway, telling myself that I was only going to make sure that Keith was out with his boys and not with some slut.

When I pulled up to the Skybox I rode around the parking lot, but when I didn't spot Keith's truck I sped off. Not knowing where he was I dialed his cellphone once again, still no answer. Growing more pissed by the second I drove past a few other spots that Keith and his boys were known to hang out at from time to time, but still no luck. Finally, after looking at the clock read twelve-thirty I decided to take my ass home. Keith would have to feel my wrath the next time that I saw him. Unlike my sister, I'm not stupid; Keith always played the Stony and Pete game with her when he was really with me. Sometimes while he was sexing me Pandia would call and he'd lie and say that he was kicking it with one of his boys and that he'd be home soon. I'm no fool, I knew that Keith was out with someone else, but who?

Deciding not to take the highway home I instead rode down Delmar; as my car neared the shop I slowed down when I noticed a car sitting out front. It was silver Ford Focus with tinted windows and Illinois plates; there was only one person who drove that car and it was Keisha. Wondering why this heifer was at the shop other than to steal products I pulled my car to the side of the building and to my surprise Keith's truck was parked in the parking lot. Furious I tried to get out of the car without putting it in park and ended up rear ending Keith's truck. Putting my own car in reverse and parking it alongside of Keith's I jumped out and walked to the side door of the salon.

Quietly putting my key in the door and turning the lock, I could hear soft moans coming from the front of the shop. I tip-toed to the front and there was Keith sitting in his wife's chair with Keisha, butt naked riding him. Her head was thrown back as she rotated her hips on my man's lap. I could taste the blood boiling in my throat as I watched the man that I loved fuck the girl that I gave a chance. I wanted to come out of the darkness and choke the life out of Keisha, but the tears forming in my eyes made impossible for me to see clearly. Keith stood up; bending Keisha over the chair he took her from behind. I couldn't believe it. I couldn't say anything because I'd expose my own skeleton, instead I walked back out into the frigid midnight air.

Before I left, I made sure Keith got a nice parting gift; I took my key and ran it along the length of his truck on the driver's side first then

Skeletons

repeated my actions on the passenger's side. I rode home with tears in my eyes and pain in my heart wondering how he could do this. How ironic, this must be how my sister felt every time that he was with me.

18
SANTANA

Gathering a stack of checks that I needed to present to Mr. gold for approval I walked out of my office passing by Tabitha's desk she winked at me and continued her telephone conversation.
"Good afternoon Julie." I smiled to Mr. Gold's young assistant.
"Good afternoon Mrs. Montgomery," she smiled, "I love your suit."
"Thanks. Is Mr. Gold in his office?"
"Yes, I told him that you were coming."
Thanking Julie I walked into Mr. Gold's office, he was standing in front of the large floor to ceiling windows with a golf putter in one hand and a scotch in his other.
"Good afternoon Santana." He grinned when he saw me.
"How are you?" I asked taking a seat on the large Italian leather couch that sat in the corner of the massive office. "I brought the checks for your approval."
Mr. Gold was a short, stout man, but what he lacked in height he more than made up in business sense as Gold's Medical Supply was the second largest medical supply company in the Midwest. "I see that you are practicing your swing." I smiled at the putter that he held.
"I can't wait until the spring so that I can hit the golf course." He smiled as he sat next to me and looked over the checks.

Shimeka R. McFadden

After he approved the checks he handed them back to me and asked, "How is your new assistant working out for you Santana?"

"Tabitha, is doing a great job; why do you ask?"

Sighing Mr. Gold said, "Well some of the other workers have said that she spends a great deal of time fraternizing with co-workers and you know how I feel about that. It's not good for business."

"I understand, but honestly I think that Tabitha has done a great job so far, but I will be sure to talk to her about socializing on the job."

"You make sure that you do that, I don't want to have to find you another assistant any time soon." He warned, "Have a good day."

When I made it back to my office I immediately called Tabitha in so that I could talk to her about my conversation with Mr. Gold. Before I could get it out she handed me a small baggie filled with multi-colored pills with a smile on her face, "This is for you."

I looked at the tiny bag and asked, "What is this?"

"Your escape." She licked her red glossed lips.

I shifted in my seat, "Before we escape, I need to talk to you about something that Mr. Gold has brought to my attention." I put the bag in my purse and looked at Tabitha, "He said that a few co-workers are complaining that you are doing too much socializing around the office."

"Socializing, you know that I'm at my desk working unless I come in here to talk to you." She said defensively.

"I know, but just to be on the safe side, please watch yourself the people in here can be devious and I don't want you to lose your job because of it."

As Tabitha began walking out of the door she turned around and said, "Let's get a drink after work."

"I wish that I could Tab, but…"

"But what? All that you are going to do is go home and do your usual boring ass routine. Come on, live a little it is just one drink and I promise that I will have you home in time to be turned down for sex by your husband."

That night after work Tabitha and I went to The Melting Pot for dinner and a few drinks and as usual Tabitha turned every head in the restaurant. As we were finishing our dinner, a bottle of wine and swallowing a pill, Tabitha leaned over to me and whispered, "You are so hot Santana, I don't know why you act like such an old woman. I would do you in a heartbeat. The son of a Preacher man is one lucky bastard."

I laughed as the pill took effect and I felt as if I were on fire.

"Thank you." I smiled. Feeling Tabitha's hand on my thigh made me jump at first then I relaxed as she moved her hand higher and higher until it

Skeletons

reached my wanting pussy.

"I won't stop until you want me to. "She whispered as she warmed my spot with her soft fingertips. "You deserve pleasure and I want to give you exactly what you deserve." She breathed into my ear as she massaged my clit through the wool trousers that I wore.

Not knowing what came over me, normally I would not have let Mike touch me like this in a public place, but Tabitha was different. Normally I wouldn't have moaned like this where other people could possibly hear, but with Tabitha I felt free.

"I want to kiss you." I whispered as I turned my face to meet her, our lips were inches away; I could taste the air that she breathed. "Your lips look like they taste soft and sweet, like butterscotch." With Tabitha I could finally say what I wanted, be who I wanted and not worry about being judged.

She laughed as she ran her tongue across her lips, "Butterscotch that is the first time that I've ever heard that one."

"Sweet like butterscotch and hot like brandy."

"Kiss me." She said leaning in.

My body felt as if I'd stuck my finger in an electrical socket as our lips touched each other; Tabitha's mouth was sweet, wet as she parted her lips, easing her tongue into my mouth, running it across my lips. Her kiss was that of strawberries and Merlot and my body was on fire. Tabitha's hand caressed the side of my face while we kissed like lovers in the rain. I didn't care who saw us, I didn't care about the stares that we got from the other patrons of the restaurant; for once in my life I was living in the moment and it felt good to be wanted.

"Come home with me." She breathed softly with her lips still touching mine.

I didn't have to say a word; my body language said it all; it said that I wanted to taste even more of Tabitha. I grabbed my wallet and paid for dinner and leaving a hefty tip. Grabbing our coats we began to walk towards the exit, and then I spotted a familiar face.

"Santana, what are you doing here?" Jovanna asked as her and Asteria sat with Londyn eating dinner.

Trying to hide the desire in my eyes I smiled, "Hey guys, I-I was just out having dinner with my assistant." I stammered as I tried to wipe Tabitha's smeared lip gloss from my lips. I could feel Tabitha shift in annoyance when I introduced her as only my assistant.

Asteria eyed Tabitha as if she knew her before she spoke, "Well aren't you going to introduce us to your friend?"

"Oh, I'm sorry, "I stammered, "Tabitha these are my friends Jovanna and

Asteria and Londyn."

"Nice to meet you all." Tabitha smiled.

"If would've known that you were here, we would've loved to join you." I smiled, trying to keep my composure.

"How long have you been working with Santana?" Asteria asked.

Tabitha threw her long hair over her shoulder and licked her lips, "Just a few weeks."

"Oh so you are another temp?" Asteria asked rather rudely.

That question made Tabitha uncomfortable, "No, I think that I'll be around for a while."

Sensing the growing tension between Tabitha and Asteria I told the girls that I had to get home and that I'd call them later. As Tabitha and I made our way out of the restaurant I couldn't help but notice the way that Asteria looked at Tabitha as if she were a familiar and unwanted face.

I followed Tabitha's yellow VW Bug to her apartment in the Central West End. I was beginning to have second thoughts and wanted to turn around and go the other direction. The thought of going home to another boring night with Mike and the kids I quickly changed my mind.

Tabitha's apartment was exactly like I'd imagined it to be, small but very nicely decorated. I sat on soft, leather couch while Tabitha made us a drink. The scent of jasmine and vanilla filled my nostrils and the sensual sounds of Trey Songz filled my ears.

Tabitha handed me a glass filled with Grey Goose and cranberry juice and sat down next to me. "This is the only drink that I know how to make." She smiled as she sipped the drink.

"Your place is nice." I said as I looked around the apartment.

"Thank you, but I bet that it is nothing compared to your house. I am only an assistant you know." She replied. Tabitha took another swig from her glass and looked at me, "Let's cut the shit Santana, I think that you are by far the sexiest woman that I've ever met and I can't help but want you."

I swiped my fallen bangs from my eyes and smiled at her, "Thank you Tabitha, but I'm married with children."

"But you aren't happy." She answered pulling my face to hers as she softly kissed me running the tip of her tongue along my lips. She tasted so good. "Let me show you happiness." She whispered taking my hand and leading me to her bedroom.

Trey's sensual voice filled the room as Tabitha slid my silk shirt over my head, unzipping my trousers and letting them fall to my ankles she ran her hands along my body stopping to graze my hard nipples with the back of her fingertips. Kissing my neck Tabitha grasped my ass through the black briefs.

"Lay back." She motioned, I did as I was told. I lay back on her soft bed as she removed her clothes. Tabitha's body belonged on a billboard, with its soft curves and smooth skin.

"I'm nervous. I experimented with another woman in college, but it has been so long ago." I confessed.

"Don't worry baby, I got you." She said as she kissed me from my neck to the top of my pubic bone. "You smell so good, but I wonder how you taste." She purred as she ran her soft, moist tongue along my bare breast with one hand while massaging my clit with the other. I was suprised how my body responded to her every touch, kiss, caress and lick. Gripping the butter-soft sheets arching my back, I bit my bottom lip trying to stifle the moans that were seeping through my mouth as she slowly ravaged my pussy with her tongue and lips.

She moaned as she moved her fingers inside of my quivering body. "Hold back with Mike, but not with me."

"Mike could never make me feel the way that you do." I moaned softly.

Tabitha took that as a cue to send me overboard and covered my pussy with her mouth and sucked until my body was overcome with so much pleasure that I called out to God, Buddha and Krishna, tearing the sheets away from the bed while my legs quivered until they fell limp. Tabitha crawled her way towards my face with a mischievous smile on her face.

"Oh my God Tabitha," I breathed, "I can't believe that you made me come. Mike never makes me come."

"You have been deprived for far too long Santana." she smiled.

Tabitha as she worked her very own brand of magic on her pussy with her fingers. Removing her hand I licked my own fingers, reached down and found her spot while I ran my tongue around the soft mound of her perfect breasts until she was shuddering moans that were sure to have woken the neighbors. Crawling on top of my exotic mistress I kissed the softness of her body making my way down to her thighs which I nibbled while she squealed in delight. Before long I was returning her favor as she gripped the pillow, scratching the mattress and calling out to the heavens while my tongue played the harp on her juicy pussy as I strummed it with precision leaving Tabitha quivering on the bed with a look of pleasure written all over her face.

"If I didn't know any better I'd say that this isn't your first time Santana." She breathed as she ran her fingers through my sandy brown hair while I rested between her legs with my head on her flat stomach.

"I have a few skeletons in my closet that most people don't know about."

"We all have skeletons." She exhaled sleepily.

I knew that I was wrong but it felt so right falling asleep with my arms and legs entangled in the softness of Tabitha's flesh as she lay next to me, our breathing in harmony with one another. It was well after midnight when I woke up and got dressed in the dark while my lady lover stayed asleep. I was amazed at how beautiful she was even as she was slumbering. I asked myself what could a woman this amazing who could get any man or woman that she wanted see in someone like me. I am far from ugly, but at the same time I was no longer in my prime, married with two children. What was it that drew Tabitha to me in the first place?

I tried sneaking into the house, but Mike was wide awake, lying in bed watching ESPN as usual. He looked at the digital disrespect on the clock that read one-forty-three in the morning then looked at me as if I were crazy.

"I'm sorry, I must have lost track of time." I said as I undressed.

"That would be believable had it come from someone who didn't make it a point at being punctual for every moment of her life." He fussed. "I called you, but it went straight to voicemail. You never turn your phone off when you are out Santana. What if something were wrong with the kids?"

"My battery ran dead." I lied.

Mike snorted, "As smart as you are, one would think that you could come up with a craftier lie than that!"

"Mike, it is late, the children are asleep and I really don't feel like an argument with you tonight. I went to dinner with Tabitha then we went back to her place and just hung out. I apologize, but I did lose track of time and my phone did die." I fussed. "If you don't trust me then that is your own issue, but I am telling you the truth." I walked into our bathroom and turned on the shower. I took my time showering not only trying to hold out for Mike to cool off and fall asleep, but also because I was not in a rush to wash Tabitha's scent off of my body.

19
JOVANNA

Ignoring the intensifying ache in my thighs I hit the plus button on the treadmill to set the incline to ten percent which made my heart pump harder and sent my heart rate soaring to the target of one hundred and ninety beats per minute. With the sounds of Busta Rhymes ringing through my ears I pounded harder and harder on the machine as if I were running from something, but like in reality I was running on a treadmill, but getting nowhere regardless of how fast I ran my problems only followed me.

Ignoring the sweat that poured down my face I picked up the pace a little; my breathing was harsh and I was beginning to lose my form which made my workout even harder. Feeling a light tap on my shoulder I looked over to find my workout partner, Asteria, looking at me with concern in her eyes.

Turning down my iPod and the pace on the treadmill I slowed down to a brisk jog and took the ear buds out of my ringing ears.

"Hey girl you are going hard over there; is everything okay?" she asked as she walked holding on to the rails.

"Yeah, I'm cool; just trying to shed a few pounds before the wedding." I lied.

I didn't want to tell her that Chad had called me three times in the past two days. I didn't want to concern her with the fact that he not only threatened my life, but also the life of my soon to be husband. I wouldn't dare tell my best friend about my past life as a stripper turned prostitute. So I lied.

"I have to be able to fit into that five-thousand-dollar Vera Wang gown by June."

"Girl you are the last person that needs to lose some weight, your body is perfect." Asteria complemented.

"My secrets are well hidden." I winked.

After our workout, Asteria and I went to lunch at Noodles & Company, but I found it difficult to concentrate while she talked about her troubles with this anonymous man that she has been dealing with. I guess she mistook my silence for me not wanting to hear her whine about him not spending the night, but my mind was in another place.

"I think that I'm going to fire Keisha." She said changing the subject.

"Really, I thought that she was doing better."

Asteria shook her head, "Her work is great, but she is too unprofessional and I'm sick of dealing with it."

"Wow that was sudden Asteria, being how all of this time when Pandia wanted to fire her, you were the one defending Keisha." I said in between bites of my salad.

"I gave her the benefit of the doubt, but now I don't see a change in things with her ghetto ass so she has got to go."

The look on my friend's face was undeniable, she wanted Keisha gone and she wanted her gone now.

"Well if you say so, but just let the girl down easy."

"I have to talk to my sister about it first, but Keisha will be gone by this time next week for sure."

Just then a familiar face walked into the restaurant; dressed flawlessly in an expensive peanut butter and tan three-piece suit with matching peanut butter fedora Chad strolled in with a Don Diego cigar perched between his thick lips.

"I'm sorry sir, but this is a non-smoking restaurant." The hostess said as she seated him two tables away from us.

"Don't worry sweetheart, I am not going to light it?" his raspy Southern accent was undeniable.

I couldn't believe my eyes as my antagonist sat only ten feet from me, I wanted to get up and run out of the door, but I didn't want to raise suspicion in Asteria so I tried to keep my cool the best that I could.

"Wow look at that zoot suit!" Asteria joked. "He sure is clean."

"Yeah that is a pretty nice suit." I managed through the huge lump of

fear that formed in my throat. "I'm finished, are you ready to go?"
Asteria couldn't take her eyes off of Chad, he held the room's attention with his good looks and Southern swagger, but I knew what kind of secrets that he had hidden in his closet. As I beckoned to the waitress to bring the check he turned towards our table and walked over, removing the fedora his devilish eyes pierced my skin sending a chill down my spine. "Good afternoon ladies." His raspy southern drawl took Asteria by surprise.

"Good afternoon," she spoke, "Nice suit I don't see many men dressed like that around here, but judging from your southern accent you aren't from around here."

"No mam I come from Memphis, Tennessee home of the blues." He smiled as he made his way towards our table.

I sat motionless unable to breathe, Asteria looked at me as if I were missing a screw in my head. Not wanting to look at his face, I glanced at the solid gold cufflinks that rested perfectly on his sleeve, my eyes making their way down at the peanut butter gators that embraced his size twelve feet. The scent of Versace Man filled the air around us as he stood close enough to touch. For what Chad lacked in morality he made up for it in presentation.

Looking at me through eyes that were as cold as the January wind in Chicago he said, "How are you?"

His dark skin was almost free of imperfections except the reminder that someone tried to kill him long ago then I remembered quickly what type of man that was standing before my friend and I. "I'm fine." I said coldly, "We were just leaving." I said as I pulled my credit card from my wallet placing it in the basket on top of the check.

"I have never been to this restaurant before, would you ladies be so kind as to recommend something to me." He asked my friend.

"I just had the pasta Fresca, but you look like a man who likes meat so I'd suggest the spaghetti and meatballs for you." Asteria suggested. "Their spaghetti is to die for, but since we just finished working out I decided on something light." She flirted as she batted her thick lashes.

"That sounds great. What did you have pretty girl?" he asked with his icy eyes piercing my skin.

"I just had a salad." I answered quickly.

"What brings a man like you to St. Louis?" Asteria asked.

"Business as usual." He smiled. "I have to get with a former business associate of mine, but this associate has been rather reluctant to meet with me."

"Well sometimes you just grab them by the throat and make them see things your way." Asteria said.

"That doesn't sound like a bad idea." He said looking directly at me.

"Hi my name is Asteria by the way." She said extending her hand.

Chad kissed the back of my unassuming friend's hand, "Nice to meet you Asteria. What an unusual name."

"Asteria is the Goddess of night and falling stars." She flirted.

"Oh I see." He said, "how poetic."

"Poetic, you are the first person to say that my name is poetic." She was already being wooed by his charm.

"What is your friend's name?" he asked her as I signed the receipt.

They waited for me to answer, instead I ignored him.

"This is Jovanna, who has seemed to have gone mute on us." She introduced me to someone that I knew all too well.

I stood in a hurry which took Asteria by surprise as she wanted to continue to flirt with danger. Chad stepped back to let me pass him, Asteria followed, but not before saying her goodbyes and handing him her business card.

"Girl what is wrong with you?" she asked as she rushed behind me trying to catch up, "I was about to get my flirt on."

"You don't even know him Asteria." I said as I put my coat on while we made our way out of the restaurant door.

"Okay, I was trying to get to know him; maybe he is just what I need to finally forget about the loser that I'm dealing with now."

"You need to be a little more careful with who you let in your bed." I put.

That last statement stopped my friend in her tracks as she stood on the passenger side of my car with her mouth handing open, "What is that supposed to mean?"

"I'm sorry, that slipped out." I apologized, "Let's just forget that I said that."

"No I don't think that I can forget that Jovanna." She fumed as she got in my car and slammed the door, "I feel as if you are judging me."

"I'm not judging you Asteria and I apologize for what I said now let's just forget it." I started up the car and pulled out of the parking lot. I knew that I had to get Chad his money and I had to do it as soon as possible.

"You know what Jovanna, I'm hurt by what you said and I don't think that I can just forget about it. Do you think that you are better than me because you are about to marry this white dude?"

"What does Justin have to do with any of this?" I asked.

"I've known you for ten years and it just seems as if since Justin asked you to marry him sometimes you act just like Pandia thinking that you are better than me."

Skeletons

"I don't think that I'm better than anyone Asteria, I was just distracted and I didn't mean to say what I originally said." I defended myself. "I'm not about to argue with you about this, I apologized and if you don't want to accept it then so be it."

Asteria looked at me through silted eyes, "I think that you'd better put the pedal to the metal Jovanna because I am feeling some sort of way right now and being that you are one of my best friends, I think that it would be best that you got me to my car as soon as possible."

We rode back to the gym in silence, when I pulled alongside Asteria's blue Avalon she opened the door and got out, "I don't know what the fuck is going on with you Jovanna, but you really need to check yourself before you lose a good friend." She slammed my car door so hard that my car rocked.

I couldn't think of Asteria as I drove home, all that I could think about was seeing Chad; how did he know that I was there? I wondered. I questioned if he'd been following me and if he knew where Justin and I lived. I looked in my rearview mirror and no one was behind me, but to be safe I took a few detours before I was comfortable enough to drive to our home in the city where my future husband awaited me.

Shimeka R. McFadden

20
ASTERIA

I couldn't believe that the bitch had the audacity to speak to me when I walked into the salon Tuesday morning. Keisha may have known how good Keith's dick felt inside of her the other night, but what she didn't know was that I was five minutes away from knocking that stupid lip piercing out of her mouth. Making it my business to speak to everyone but her I held my head high as I strutted to the back office where I contemplated on how I was going to fire her crooked ass.
"Hey girl what's up, I got your text." Pandia said when she came into the office to put her coat away. My sister looked as if she hadn't slept in days Keith was putting her through hell and for that I felt terrible.
"I think that we should fire Keisha." I put bluntly.
My sister looked suprised, "Wow that was random; I thought that you were her number one fan."
"Well I changed my mind she is not working out as I once thought and she needs to be let go immediately."
Pandia sat down across from me, "Tell me the real reason Asteria."
"The real reason is that the bitch is unprofessional as hell and I'm tired of having to correct her mistakes the other stylists are starting to complain about her. It's not like she has dedicated clients so losing her won't hurt the salon at all."

"You know I've never liked the girl in the first place, but if we fire her that will leave an unoccupied chair in the salon and we need that rent money Asteria."

My sister was right, we needed to keep someone in that station at all times. "It won't be a problem getting someone back in that station; there are stylists graduating from beauty schools all of the time and those people are looking for a chair and an opportunity."

Pandia tapped her unkempt nails on the glass-top desk and sucked her teeth while she thought it over, "You are right Asteria, let's move forward and let her go, but since this was your great idea I'll let you handle it." She said as she stood to go out to her station where she had a client waiting.

I couldn't wait to call that bitch in to my office and fire her ass.

Looking in the mirror I admired all of the hard work that I'd put in at the gym because unlike my sister I refused to get out of shape just because I had a baby. I kept my stomach flat, my ass and legs were tight as a runner's and my arms weren't flabby. Since I owned a salon I made sure that my hair stayed on point and I never had chipped nail polish on my feet or fingertips. I hate to be conceited, but a bitch looked good that is why it is hard to fathom why Keith would want to fuck around with a sloppy, broke bitch like Keisha.

I kept myself busy with paperwork until after lunch when I stepped out of the office and noticed that Keisha was sitting in her styling chair waiting on a client but this time she didn't have the usual sour look on her face, this time she looked happy.

"Keisha, do you mind if I have a word with you?" I asked.

She got up from her chair and followed me into my office; I was feeling good about myself.

"Have a seat." Keisha plopped down in the chair and looked at me with a slight smirk on her face.

"Keisha, you have come a long way here and I'm rather suprised at how much you have learned. Your hair cutting and styling techniques have improved greatly in the past six months."

Keisha looked at me blankly, "And…"

"And, unfortunately with all of the improving that you have done you still lack the professionalism that it takes to work in a salon of this caliber. With that being said, I'm sorry, but I'm going to have to let you go."

Keisha's laugh took me by surprise. "You are something else Asteria." She chuckled.

Growing angry and confused I asked, "What?"

"Please tell me that you are not firing me because I had a little piece of

Keith the other night."

I looked at her in astonishment.

"If that is the case then Pandia should have fired your scandalous ass a long time ago." She continued.

Swallowing hard I rose from my throne of power, but felt as small as peasant. "Excuse me?"

Keisha smiled, showing off a set of teeth that were in need of dental work. "I saw you watching us the other night and I hope that you like what you saw." Standing, she moved towards me "Keith is amazing, you have no idea how many times he made me come. Well come to think of it you do know, being how it is that you have been fucking your sister's husband for the past three years and all. I wonder how well you sleep at night?"

Resisting the urge to slap Keisha back into her mother's womb, I quietly listened as she went on.

"Now if I were you, I wouldn't want my sister or my friends and family to know how devious I am so it might be in your best interest to let me get back to work." Keisha winked at me with thick baby doll lashes and strutted out of the office, leaving me standing there with my mouth hanging open.

How did she know that I was watching them that night, I was certain that I was well hidden in the darkness of the salon. Furthermore, how did she know that Keith and I were seeing one another all of this time? Pissed off I grabbed my cellphone and dialed Keith's number, but as usual he let it ring to voicemail. Hanging up I sat in my office for the rest of the day, not wanting to be bothered by anyone.

"You know that was real fucked up what you did to my truck the other night." Keith said as he walked into my house. Still wearing his brown police uniform; it use to turn me on to see him in uniform, but tonight he sickened me. Many nights we played cop and robber while he was still in uniform having sex in the backseat of his squad car. He scooped Latif into his arms and kissed my son on his forehead.

"How is my little man?" He played with my son as I looked at him through hateful eyes. "What is the matter now?" Keith asked when he put Latif back down to play with his toys.

I slapped Keith across his face as hard as I could, "How dare you!" I spat. "I saw you fucking Keisha last night you dirty bastard." I fought hard to keep the tears from my eyes.

Keith touched to the side of his face with one hand and he grabbed me around my throat with the other. Pushing my back against the living room wall knocking a picture of Latif and I onto the floor where it shattered scaring my son who started to scream. I tried fighting him back, but I was no match for Keith as he was much stronger than I was. "I don't give a fuck who you think you are and I don't give a damn if that little boy is mine or not, but I do know that if you ever in your life put your hands on me again, you will regret it from your hospital bed!" he spat in my face slamming my head against the wall.

Holding my throat I screamed at the man who I wanted to spend the rest of my life with, the man whom I betrayed my own twin sister for, "Get out of my house and don't you ever come back!"

Keith bent down and kissed our crying son on his forehead, "Don't worry little man, your momma is just tripping, I'll be back later on."

Keith looked at me with contempt written all over his face as he turned to walk out of the door leaving me crying and alone with no one to talk to because no one would ever understand. Latif came to me as I sat on the floor and kissed me softly on my face, I held on to my son as he was the only person who loved me because at this point I didn't even love myself.

21
SANTANA

Mike's eyes felt as if they were peering into my soul as I shifted uncomfortably in my seat during Sunday morning service at New Life Church of God In Christ where his father, Pastor Lewis Montgomery, was preaching a powerful sermon. Trying to ignore him and pretend that everything was normal I said a few "Amen" and "Thank you Jesus!" along with the rest of the congregation.
"Malik, sit still baby, grandpa is almost finished." I instructed in a whisper to our son.
"But I have to pee." He grumbled.
"Well you will have to wait; you know that you can't get up during the sermon." Mike responded sternly.
"Yes sir." Our son pouted.
Mike's father was a small man with a big voice and when he spoke he took control of the room. Mike and his father looked exactly alike with dark, curly hair, deep-set brown eyes that sat below thick perfectly arched eyebrows. The only thing that was different was that Mike was at least a six inches taller than his five foot-five father and since Mike worked out a lot he had a more athletic build than his stocky father.
Wiping the sweat off of his saturated brow Pastor continued, "In closing I want to read a passage from Revelation 20:12; and I saw the dead,

great and small, standing before the throne, and books were opened, which is the book of life. And the dead were judged by what was written in the books, according to what they had done." Taking off his bifocals he closed his Bible and looked directly at the congregants, "Be careful of the skeletons which hide in your closets while you can hide them from your loved ones, you cannot hide them from God." With that he ended the service.

After the sermon we walked up to Mike's parents and embraced them. I loved Mike's parents, they were such good and kind people and they raised Mike and his sister very well. I wished that my own parents were as loving as Mike's, instead my mother and father were too wrapped up in their own lives to even call me every once in a while to see how I was doing.

"How are you son?" Pastor Lewis asked hugging Mike.

"We are doing good dad." Mike lied, "That was a powerful sermon that you preached today."

"Yes it was, yes it was; secrets can only be kept for so long until those skeletons start peeking their heads out of the closet." He said in his deep voice.

I pretended to adjust my purse strap upon my shoulder.

"Grandpa, when did you need me to come by and put the plastic on the window?" Malik asked.

"You can come over right after you get changed this afternoon." Mother answered. "You did a fantastic job on the basement Malik."

"How have you been Santana?" Pastor asked.

"I've been good, I wanted to bring you and mother some of my chili that I made the other night, but I ran out of the house and forgot the container so I'll bring you some when I drop Malik off this afternoon."

My phone vibrated insided of my purse, glancing down at the screen I saw that it was from Tabitha. Instantly my body temperature rose and I felt a tingling sensation between my thighs.

I still taste your sweet pussy on my lips.

Smiling I put the phone back in my purse noticing that Mike was looking at me with an intense look on his face.

"That was another raunchy forward from Asteria; that girl is something else." I lied and my husband didn't buy what I was selling.

"Grandma can I come to your house with Malik today?" Mya asked as she held on to Mother's hand.

"If that is alright with your parents." Mother said looking directly at Mike who was too preoccupied with looking at me.

"Sure that is fine, she can come over just as long as she stays out of her

Skeletons

brother's way." I answered.

A few church members stepped up to speak with the Pastor and First Lady, so Mike and I excused ourselves and walked outside to the car.

Still feeling the effects from last night, I fell asleep on the ride home while Mike and the kids talked about sports as usual.

I loved Mike, but I questioned if I was still in love with him. Things between us had gotten to be so predictable and dry that I often felt as if we were brother and sister rather than husband and wife. Mike use to entice and excite me, he use surprise me with breakfast in bed, candle light dinners and roses delivered to my office in the middle of the afternoon. Those things seemed liked years ago, now I barely get a card on my birthday or Mother's Day. Last Christmas he gave me cash as if I were his damn niece instead of his wife. Tabitha brought excitement back into my life, with her I didn't feel like Mike's wife Santana; with Tabitha I felt like a new person, a person with passion, a person with desire and a person who was not predictable.

When we got home the kids went up to their rooms to change clothes so Mike could take them to his parent's house. I went into the kitchen to make a snack for everyone, Mike followed.

"What did you really think about today's sermon?" he questioned as he loosened his tie and threw it on the island.

"I thought that it was an interesting message that needed to be said." I responded moving the tie from the island and placing it back in his hand. "Put this in the laundry room."

"I agree there are some skeletons in people's closets that just need to come out but when they do…well I'm sure that you know where I'm coming from." He said then walked upstairs to change clothes.

Taking my phone out of my purse I read Tabitha's message again then hit the delete button just in case Mike decided to snoop through my cellphone.

Mike came to bed that night and attempted to put his arms around me, what usually felt normal and comforting now felt annoying and wrong.

"Baby what is going on with you?" he asked, "I don't want to fight, but you have been acting strange lately and I can't help but think that you have another man in your life."

Turning over on my back I fumed, "Mike you should know me better than that but if I did have another man you need to stop and ask yourself why it is that I chose to disrespect our marriage vows in the first place."

"Baby I'm trying everything in my power to make you happy, but when you don't communicate with me how do I know what is going on."

"I do communicate with you, but a major part of the communication process is listening and I can't help that you don't do that very well."

Mike let out a hurt sigh, "Now you insult me."

Sitting up in our king sized sleigh bed, I looked at Mike in disbelief, "On one hand you want me to communicate and tell you what is wrong but as soon as I do that you get offended. That is exactly why this whole conversation is pointless."

"How can something that can benefit our marriage be pointless Santana?" he asked with pleading eyes.

"Look I'm tired and we both have to work in the morning." I gave up while rubbing my temples in frustration, "Let's just get some sleep." I turned my body away from him and pulled the covers up to my ears. I knew that Mike was hurt, but at this point it was time for me to do me, it was time for me to be selfish.

22

JOVANNA

I couldn't breathe; my flailing arms were growing limp by every second that passed; I felt my eyes struggling to stay open, but that too was a fight that I was losing. Gasping for air, I fought my assailant to get loose, but I felt my life slipping away as my soul began to prepare itself for the next journey. Chad's hands felt like vice grips around my neck, the uncaring look in his grey eyes was as emotionless as the blade that lay stuck in my back. I was dying a slow and painful death, in the background I could hear Justin's pleading voice calling out for me by my name, Marquita.

Waking up from my nap I was drenched in sweat, my breaths were deep and jagged. Jumping up from the couch I ran into the bathroom and threw cold water on my face. Looking at my red, swollen eyes I could still feel his hands around my throat, choking the life out of me. I knew Chad, and I knew that he would not give up until I gave him what he wanted. I now regretted what happened the night that I thought I left my past behind me.

Wishing that I could take back my past, I knew that I had to make right what I did wrong over ten years ago, but in order to do that I would have to contact Chad and that was something that I was not prepared to do.

Shimeka R. McFadden
July 1999

The Memphis heat was sweltering; I grabbed my spray bottle and spritzed water on my face and body in an attempt to cool down. Even though it was well past midnight, the temperature was still in the mid nineties. Standing outside of the Centennial Inn on Shelby Street, my feet were starting to ache; I didn't know what was taking Chad so long to get here, the job was over an hour and a half ago.

Chad had been acting really funny towards me since he found out about me taking G.E.D classes during the day.

Chad causally pulled up to the front of the motel as if he were on time, rolling my eyes I got inside of the candy-apple red Cadillac which was paid for with money earned on the backs of his women. The stench of the Don Diego cigar smoke filled my nostrils and lungs and I coughed. "It took you long enough." I fussed underneath my breath.

Not saying so much as hello, Chad held out his soft hands to accept the stack of fresh bills that I laid in his palm. Slamming ten, fresh twenty-dollar bills in his hands I folded my arms across my breast waiting as he counted every single bill as if I couldn't be trusted. I knew better than to skim money off the top, I'd seen girls get beat down from trying to steal money from Chad.

Loving Chad came so easily when I was a wide-eyed seventeen-year-old, run-away who was looking for someone to love. My parents were too fucked up to give a care, both too strung out on crack to even know that I ran away. When he found me working at the Honey Lounge he was my escape from a place that I had to drink or smoke weed in order to get up on stage. He took me away from all of that, his words were so smooth that he drew me in and I never wanted to leave him. First he made love to my mind, then he made love to my body and I was in love with him.

Loving Chad came easily because he treated me better than any of the men that came to the Honey Pot; he even treated me better than my own parents. Chad was more than my pimp, he was more than my boyfriend, he was even more than my husband; Chad was like my father and he taught me the tricks of my trade like a child learned to ride the bike from her father. I hung on to his every word as if he was a God and I was his follower. Now that love that I felt for him was gone, replaced by hatred and disgust.

The smooth words that he used to say to get me to do whatever he wanted now I didn't even listen when he talked. His touch was so loving and caring at one point, but now I couldn't even stand the smell of him or his foul smelling cigars. As much as I hated Chad, I knew that he had

a hold on me and unless I left him I would be stuck with him until I stopped earning him money. I knew that I had to get away from him.
Tasha was one of the girls that worked for Chad; we lived in a two bedroom apartment around the corner from him. Chad was so insecure in himself that he had to have complete control over every aspect of our lives. Not only where we lived, but also what we ate as he brought all of our groceries, what we wore as he took us shopping and every time we left the house as if we left the house without him knowing we would pay for it later. I was twenty-two and I felt sorry for Chad, he was a sad and pitiful excuse for a man and I couldn't wait to leave him.
"I am tired of this shit Tasha!" I fussed right after Chad dropped me off that night.
Looking up from polishing her toes Tasha said, "What is going on?"
"Not only did this fat fuck of a trick spit his foul tasting come all on my face, but Chad took his sweet time picking me up tonight!"
"Be careful of what you say Marquita," my friend warned as she looked towards Sunny and Lacy's room, "You never know who will snitch."
Sunny and Lacy were two of Chad's other girls and they hated Tasha and me because we got the higher end clients and they looked for every chance they got to snitch on us.
Rolling my eyes I continued, "I don't even care anymore Tasha, it's not like Chad hasn't kicked my ass enough already. To add insult to injury he won't even let us see a dime of the money that we earn."
Taking the wig off, I tossed it across the room, "I'm just tired of working my ass off and not having anything to show for it. Yet this slimy mother fucker walks around in five-hundred dollar suits, three-hundred dollar gators and one-hundred dollar hats! I swear if I could get my hands on that money that he keeps in his safe…."
Tasha quickly looked up at me and closed our bedroom door, "What money in what safe?" my usually loud-mouthed friend whispered.
"Chad keeps our money in a safe that is hidden in his closet at his house."
"Have you seen it with your own eyes because I've never been inside of his apartment?"
At one point I was one of Chad's personal girls so he would invite me to spend some time with him in his apartment so I knew where almost everything was.
"Yes I'd seen it with my own eyes girl," I told my wide-eyed friend, "Every time a girl would pay him he would put the money in that safe. There has to be over ten-thousand dollars in there at one time."
"Wow girl, we'd better stop talking about this before we get into some kind of trouble." She said nervously.

In deep thought for the rest of the night, I showered then got in bed and I whispered to Tasha, "I'm going to get my money even if I have to step over that bastard's dead body to get it."

23

SANTANA

Tabitha made me want her even more than my fantasies already did. Pulling away our breathing was shallow as we reluctantly released our embrace as not to get caught while we were in the elevator.

"I bet Mike doesn't make you feel like that." She smiled, "I also know that your panties are drenched."

"I feel like I peed on myself, but I could feel how hard your nipples were through your shirt."

We giggled like two school girls until the elevator opened and Mr. Gold and his assistant walked in.

"Good morning Mrs. Montgomery." He addressed me, ignoring Tabitha.

"Good morning Mr. Gold." I spoke, "Good morning Julie." I addressed his assistant.

Tabitha, feeling disrepected, stepped up to Mr. Gold with her hand extended, "Hello Mr. Gold I don't think that we've been formally introduced, my name is Tabitha Gray."

Halfheartedly Mr. Gold shook Tabitha's hand; I had to admit that she had balls to approach him. "Nice to finally meet you Tabitha." He said, "I hope that you are keeping a professional profile while you are here."

"I always keep a professional profile Mr. Gold; maybe you haven't seen

my resume." Tabitha said through silted eyes.
"Professionalism is very important and if you want to stay in this company always remember that." He continued. "Fraternization amongst employees is strictly prohibited we are here to work not play." Tabitha looked uncomfortable for the rest of the ride to our floor where we got off and said goodbye to Mr. Gold and Julie.
"Did he really have to treat me like that?" she huffed as we walked to my office.
"That is just how Mr. Gold is, always has been and always will be don't be offended."
"Whatever, but thanks for having my back." She rolled her eyes and went to her desk where she stayed for the rest of the day.
Mr. Gold called an impromptu meeting to discuss some of the expense accounts which he and Julie have been watching closely that he wanted copies of everyone's receipts for the month. After the meeting I headed back to my office, but noticed Tabitha crying as I passed her desk. Not wanting to disturb her I walked past her as if I didn't notice and sat at my desk. A moment later my phone rang,
"This is Santana." I answered with my eye toward the door waiting for Tabitha to come in as she normally did.
"Santana Montgomery?" the female on the other end asked.
"Yes, how may I help you?"
"You can't help me, but I can help you." She said, her voice was light and airy almost childlike, but filled with pain.
"Excuse me?"
"Tabitha is not who she appears to be, you better watch your back, better yet you'd better watch your bank account." She spoke.
"I'm sorry, but who is this?"
Click. The phone went dead.

Riding home that evening I kept a close watch on the rearview mirror wondering who the strange women that called me and how she knew about Tabitha and I. When I got home, Mike and the kids wanted to go to The Olive Garden for dinner since I didn't feel like cooking anyway I decided that it was a great idea. For the first night in a long time Mike and I actually talked and laughed like we use to, but it was still in front of the children that we connected. The problem was that I don't want to connect with him as mother and father; I wanted to connect with him as husband, wife and lovers.
During dinner my cellphone rang, it was Tabitha I left the table telling Mike and the kids that I had to take the call.

Skeletons

"I'm sorry about earlier." She said. "It is just that I had a bad morning already and Mr. Gold just made it worse. He made me feel like I am nothing." She explained. "All of my life I've had to put up with people shitting on me and treating me as if I am nothing."

"That is okay, you can't let what that old fool says disrupt your entire day like that Tabitha." I said, "Is that why you were crying at your desk this afternoon?"

She was silent for a moment, "I didn't mean for you to see that."

"What was the matter Tabitha?" I asked truly concerned.

"I may have my car repossessed." She said.

"Repossessed, but why?" I asked.

"Because I can't pay my car note due to being out of work for three months before I started working for you."

"They are not willing to work with you?" I asked.

"Yeah right not in this day and age." She scoffed, "But don't worry about it I will find a way." She said.

"You can't be without your car honey; is there anyone that you can borrow the money from? Your parent's maybe."

She laughed, "Girl I haven't seen my parents in years. To them I was never good enough that is the reason that I moved to St. Louis in the first place."

"I know the feeling of not having supportive parents." I said thinking of my own.

"Maybe I can sell some of my jewelry or clothes to get the fifteen-hundred dollars that I need in order to keep my car."

"No, don't sell your things Tabitha."

"How else can I get the money?" she asked.

"I will let you borrow it and you can pay me back whenever you can."

"No I couldn't take that much money from you Santana." She gasped.

"It is a loan and besides I can't see you without your car."

"St. Louis buses run all day then and is the Metrolink."

"Don't worry about it sweetie, I'll give you the money tomorrow morning."

She began to cry, "Thank you so much Santana, you are such a good friend."

"No problem. I am out to dinner with Mike and the kids so I'll see you in the morning."

"Okay, thank you so much."

Mike eyed me as I sat back at the table, "Was that Mr. Gold?" he asked.

"No, it was Asteria and her boy troubles as usual." I lied.

Mike may have paid for dinner that night, but by the look on his face he

Shimeka R. McFadden
did not buy the lie that I was selling.

24
ASTERIA

I had not talked to Keith since the night he left my house over a week ago. He wouldn't answer my calls, texts or emails and as much as I hated him for cheating on me with Keisha I hated not being able to at least talk to him. On the outside I seemed perfectly fine, but inside I was dying without him. I missed his touch, his kiss and the way he sent me to the moon with each stroke of his dick. Every time I thought of him and Keisha together I wanted to throw up. I couldn't believe that he would betray me like this.

Every day that I walked into work Keisha made it her business to smile and speak to me as if her ass were not sleeping with my man. Pandia questioned me on why I changed my mind on firing her and I just told her that I was going to give the girl one more chance to improve.

Saturday was my day off so I went shopping with Jovanna and Santana meeting them at the Galleria in Clayton which was not too far from my house and the salon.

I hugged Santana before I looked at Jovanna; I was still pissed off at her for what she had the nerve to say to me the last time we were together. "Hey Asteria, I'm sorry for how I came at you the last time." She said, "I was bogus and out of line for what I said to you. I'm under a lot of pressure and I took it out on the wrong person."

Smiling I hugged my best friend, "It's cool girl, I figured that you were stressing about the wedding."

Santana looked confused, "Are you guys keeping secrets now?"

We all laughed, "Now we just had some silly ass words between us. It is squashed now." I said.

"I was about to say because we have been friends with one another for far too long to be keeping secrets."

"You guys know everything there is to know about me so I have nothing to hide." Jovanna smiled.

"Yeah, the two of you know me better than my own husband." Santana added.

"Best friends never keep secrets from one another." I said knowing that my own skeleton wanted to come out of the closet.

After shopping we had lunch at The Cheesecake Factory then parted ways. Pulling up to my house I was amazed to see Keith's squad car parked in its usual hiding space behind the building next to the huge oak tree.

The smell of his cologne was in the air as I walked in and sat my bags down at the door.

"What are you doing here?" I asked as I walked into my bedroom seeing him lying across my bed watching television.

"Where is Latif?" he asked.

"With your wife, why?"

"I see that you've been out spending more money."

Rolling my eyes at him I began to take off my coat and boots, "If you came to see my son you need to go home because that is where he is."

"I came to see you." He said as he walked towards me wearing nothing but a pair of Sean John boxer briefs. "Did you miss me?" I could not help but notice the huge bulge that threatened to be released from his underwear.

I wanted to tell him no and to go to Keisha's house, but my tongue wouldn't cooperate with my mind so I whispered, "Yes."

Grabbing my ponytail Keith pulled my mouth to his and gave me all of his tongue while unbuttoning my pants with his other hand. My body was his for the taking no matter how much my mind wasn't.

"Are you still seeing Keisha?" I breathed as we lay naked next to one another in pools of our own juices and sweat.

"No."

"Is that why you are here?"

"I missed you Asteria."

Skeletons

"You really hurt me Keith; how could you do that to me and with that hood rat of all people."

"What I did with Keisha had nothing to do with you, just as what I do with you has nothing to do with Pandia."

"Keith do you even love me?" I asked through the lump in my throat.

"Why do you ask me shit like that?" He said rolling over to begin his usual ritual of leaving me after he satisfied himself.

"Because I don't know how you feel about me; you know exactly how I feel about you. I gave you a son, yet you won't even give me your heart!" I cried.

"This is exactly why I didn't want to come over here. This type of shit is why I fuck with hood rats like Keisha, because they know where they stand with me and bitches like her know when to shut the fuck up!"

"Look Asteria," he said as he sat on my bed with his head in his hands, "I cannot do this any longer."

"What do you mean?" I exclaimed jumping out of bed naked.

"I mean that if this is how it is going to be then I'm done with this whole thing. We shouldn't have even started this shit in the first place!" Keith began putting on his clothes.

"Keith, but I love you is it wrong of me to want you to love me too? Is it wrong of me to want you to give me all of you just as I give you all of me?"

"I cannot give you all of me Asteria!" he yelled, "I am married to your twin sister! Why is that so hard for you to get through your head?"

"How hard was it for you to have walked away from this three years ago?" I yelled back with tears streaming down my face.

"I never meant for it to have happened, I never meant for us to have taken things this far."

Grabbing him by his hands I pulled myself to Keith and kissed him on his thick lips, his soft cheeks and his warm forehead, "But we have lasted for a reason, we are meant to be together Keith. You said it yourself that you are not in love with my sister. You said that you would leave her and that we would finally be together as a family. You said those things to me. I believed you and I've waited for you."

Looking at me in disbelief, "Asteria, that is your sister don't you even care about what that would do to her? She is the only family that you have left!"

"Pandia has it all Keith, she always has. I don't have shit, but I don't care," I cried, "All that I want is you."

Pulling away from me Keith continued to get dressed, but I stopped him, pushing him onto the bed while I climbed on top of him.

Shimeka R. McFadden

"I want you to want me too." I said as I kissed him passionately. I knew that Keith didn't love me and that he would never leave my sister, but at this point I was willing to get in where I fit in for my man even if that meant sharing him with every woman in St. Louis.

25

JOVANNA

Justin spoon-fed me ice cream while we cuddled on the couch watching a scary movie. Chad called me several times during my shopping date with Santana and Asteria, but I hit ignore every time. Since I changed the number on our home phone we didn't get any more late night calls. Chad was not playing he wanted his money and he didn't care what he had to do to get it.

"Can you believe that in four months we will be Mr. and Mrs. Justin Thompson?" he smiled kissing me on the cheek.

"I can't wait."

"I am glad that you finally took some time off of work to relax and spend some time with me. I was starting to miss you Jo."

Smiling I said, "I was missing you too Justin, I missed eating ice cream in the middle of winter with you."

Justin put the bowl on the table and began tickling me, "I see that you have jokes!"

I laughed so hard that I couldn't breathe as he tickled and kissed me all over my half naked body.

"I love you Jovanna." He said kissing me passionately.

"I just wished that your family loved me too." I sighed.

"You are not marrying them, you are marrying me."

"I know, but I still would like to have a good relationship with them, but because I'm black they act like I'm no good."

Justin sighed and sat back on the couch, "They are small minded people who are holding on old fashioned values that mean nothing in this day and age. There are plenty of interracial couples now days."

"What if we have children, they won't have grandparents on either side."

"You are right, since your parents are dead and my parents are dumb."

"That makes me kind of sad Justin." I pouted. "Maybe we shouldn't have kids."

"You don't get off that easily; I'm knocking you up as soon as I get that ring on your finger." He smiled.

Leaning over I kissed my future husband until I heard a knock on the front door, instantly my heart sank.

"I'll get it." Justin got off of the couch and walked over to the door. Looking out of the window there was a mail truck parked in front of the house. "Hey it is a certified letter for you." He said tossing me the manila envelope.

"I wonder who this is from." I said as I looked for the return address.

"Open it and find out. I'm going to the bathroom." He said as he made his way to the backroom.

My eyes widened as I thumbed through the photos in the envelope; in my hand I held two photos of a younger me dancing at the Honey Lounge. I remember who those pictures were taken as a promotional sign for the club. On the last photo there was a message written in thick black ink:

A PICTUE IS WORTH A THOUSAND WORDS, BUT THIS ONE IS WORTH TEN-THOUSAND. I WANT MY MONEY BY THE END OF THE WEEK OR SNOWFLAKE WILL FIND OUT WHO HE IS REALLY MARRYING.

Shaking, I tore the pictures up into pieces and threw them and the envelope in the fireplace then lit a fire. Just as the fire grew Justin walked out of the bathroom, "So what was in the envelope?"

"Just some promotional junk, I tossed it into the fire. I have no desire to see anything that has to do with work for a while." I managed a smile.

"Are you alright honey? You look like you seen a ghost."

"I'm fine Justin; let's get finished with what we started." I said as I walked seductively towards him.

"I think that it would be a better idea if we held off for the night, that ice cream did a number on my stomach."

"Gross nasty butt!" I laughed smacking him on his ass.

As we settled back on the couch and began watching the movie my mind wandered back to when I was known as Marquita, and the day that changed my life forever.

August 1999

It had been almost one month since I told Tasha about the safe that was hidden in Chad's bedroom closet, but I knew that she had not forgotten. she said that she wanted out just as bad as I did and we devised a plan to get the money from Chad without anyone else knowing.

It was almost nine o'clock in the morning when Tasha and I left our apartment, we told Sunny and Lacey that I was going to class and Tasha was going to do laundry. Since they stayed so high they didn't question anything of us leaving. We were silent in our own thoughts as we walked to Chad's house. I could sense regret in Tasha, but I was determined to go through with my plan even if it would cost me my life.

"What are you doing here?" Chad asked when he opened the door to me standing there. The plan was for Tasha to hide behind the bushes until I made it inside then I'd make sure the door remained unlocked so that she could enter.

"I just wanted to talk to you daddy." I answered with a smile on my face.
"This early Marquita?" he asked looking around to make sure that I was alone.

When I entered his home I stepped out of my heels before walking on the plush, blue carpet. Chad was still in his night clothes as he walked towards his bedroom, I made sure to leave the door unlocked for Tasha to enter.

"What is going on this early in the morning that made you want to come and talk to me?" he asked as he lay down on the king-sized bed.

"I just missed you, I know that things have been kind of strange between the two of us lately and I wanted to just come and lay with you like I use to do."

"Did you miss daddy?" he asked as he wrapped his big arms around my body when I laid next to him.

"Yes." I answered, fighting the urge to vomit.

"Show daddy how much you missed him." Chad said as he lay back on his back, pulling down the silk pajama pants exposing his small dick.

"*Where are you Tasha?*" I thought as I began to kiss and lick his foul-tasting member, "*Please girl don't make me have to do this by myself.*"

Needless to say, Tasha never came.

When Chad finished he fell asleep and I laid there angry not only at Tasha, but also at myself for giving Chad another piece of me. I knew that if I didn't take what was mine and leave right now, I never would.

Getting up out of bed I walked into the kitchen and grabbed a knife hiding it behind my back. Chad was snoring when I got back into the room, I tip-toed to the large closet that was filled with expensive suits and shoes. My nerves made me want to heave all of what Chad made me swallow, but I held my own as my eyes darted frantically around the closet in search of the black safe.

There it was to my right, behind several shoe and hat boxes. My hands shook as I moved the boxes to the side and pulled on the handle to the safe hoping that it was unlocked, but it wasn't. Looking at the electronic keypad I tried to think of number that Chad would have used to unlock the safe. First I tried his birthday 041071, but that didn't work. Then I tried the digits of his pager number 559871 but again that didn't work. Wiping the sweat that was pouring down my face, I thought of what his pin number would have been something that was important to Chad. Then I got an idea: 7467 or PIMP and it opened. However, just as I opened the safe I heard,

"What in the fuck are you doing?" Chad was standing behind me naked as the day that he was born; he grabbed me by my hair pulling me out of the closet. "You stupid bitch! You think that you can steal from me and get away with it!" I tried to get away from the grasp that he had on my hair, but he threw me into the dresser hitting my head.

Chad then grabbed me by my throat and began choking me as a clawed at his face. He only let me go when I put my fingers into his eyes and tried to scratch his eyeballs out, breaking off two of my nails in the process. Grabbing his eyes Chad backed off of me and rolled onto his side in pain.

"You better run bitch because if I catch you I'm going to bury you out back with my dead dog!" he yelled. Coughing and holding my throat I managed to stagger back to the closet towards the safe. I hurried as I could hear Chad coming towards me with the force of a linebacker he tackled me to the floor inside of the closet. I kicked my feet frantically, kicking him in the face a few times as he grabbed for me legs. Chad was stronger than he appeared, but I was not weak and I was not going to allow him to kill me without a fight.

He turned me over to my back, punching me across the face. I screamed as he pulled my hair and slammed my head into the softness of the carpet. I thought that I would lose consciousness, but the thick carpet acted as padding to the hard floor underneath.

"Say your prayers bitch!" he said as he began choking me again, I reached inside of the safe and grabbed the long knife landing it into Chad's side. He called out in pain as his grip loosened around my neck and he fell to the floor.

Laughing at my trembling hands as I held onto the knife he said, "Bitch if you are tough enough to use it you'd better kill me because if I get up I'm coming for you."

In the pit of my stomach I knew that Chad meant what he said as he lay on the floor holding his injured and bloodied side. I felt a sense of power as I stood over my adversary with the long blade in my hands.

"Who is the bitch now, bitch?" I spat blood from my mouth onto the carpet as he lay cowering on the floor with blood with a pool of blood underneath him. "You better kill me." He whimpered.

"You've done nothing but take from me since the first day that I met you, but you no longer hold control over me. Today is a new day, today is the day that I make you my bitch and today is the day that I take back what is due to me!" I ran over to him and hit him over the head with the butt of the knife twice until he fell asleep on the carpet lying in a puddle of his own blood. As his body hit the floor I looked in the mirror at the crazed manic that stared back at me. I was covered in blood, but for once I was not terrified. I felt liberated.

Grabbing a plastic bag I went back to the safe making sure that I kept a close eye on Chad while he lay knocked out on the carpet. I filled the bag with stacks of our money, but I didn't take it all, just what was due to me. I used one of his luxury suit jackets to wipe the blood from my face and arms, and then I tossed it to the floor next to him. Looking around his house which at one time meant so much to me, I thought that this would be the last time that I would ever see this place and Chad again.

Rushing back to the apartment, I noticed Tasha was sitting on her bed with tears streaming down her face. When she saw me and my battered face she embraced me tightly.

"I'm sorry girl, but I was scared."

"Don't worry about it." I said as I took two stacks of cash out of the bag and put it in her hands, "Take this, but I have to go Tasha."

"Where is Chad?"

I looked at her blankly, "He is still at home and I have to go."

"Take me with you." She pleaded.

"No, you have to go your own way."

"Where are you going?" she asked as I grabbed a few pieces of clothing out of my closet and stuffed them into my book bag. My hands trembling from fear.

Tasha hugged me one last time, "Take care of yourself Marquita." She whispered.

I rushed out of the house and ran to the bus stop with only what I could carry in the book bag on one arm. When I got on the bus, people looked at my bruise-covered face, shook their head then looked the other direction not waiting to get involved. I went to the Greyhound station and boarded the first bus to anywhere U.S.A. which took me to St. Louis, far away from Marquita, Chad, Tasha and my past.

26
SANTANA

I rolled my eyes as Mike's sloppy tongue danced around my clit and he fumbled with my breast like a teenaged boy. He was not as skilled as Tabitha when it came to pleasing me; in the little time I'd been sleeping with her she knew my body far better than Mike whom I'd been sleeping with since high school.
"What is wrong Santana?" he asked as he made his way up my body and kissed me on my neck, "That use to drive you wild."
"Nothing is wrong Mike." I lied. "I guess that I'm just tired."
"That is like the fifteenth time I've heard that excuse this week."
"It is nice to know that you've been keeping track." I huffed.
"I want to make love to you, is that alright?"
Mike's dick could not do what Tabitha's fingers could as he slid inside of me. He didn't make me tremble, he didn't make me sweat and as usual he didn't make me come. As he made love to me I moaned with thoughts of Tabitha running through my mind. I yearned for the softness of her skin, the firmness of her breasts and the tender way in which she kissed and bit me. Mike was too busy getting his own satisfaction to even notice that I was not getting any. I didn't care, I just want him to get finished so that I could get some sleep and wake up to see Tabitha at work in the morning.

Tabitha showed me how grateful she was for the money that I loaned her to pay her car note by cooking me dinner at her home then we had dessert in her bedroom. Covering me in chocolate sauce, strawberry sauce and whipped cream Tabitha took her time licking every morsel off of me while I squealed in delight with every stroke of her tongue. Tabitha and I had become so close while Mike and I drifted further apart. I began to distance myself from the man that I married and the children that I gave birth to. Tabitha was my new family and her friends were my friends. I felt alive in ways that I had not felt in a very long time.

We tried to keep our distance at work, but it was very hard when every time Tabitha walked into my office I wanted to touch her in some way. I couldn't help it I was captivated by her presence. However, I was still disturbed by the anoymous phone call that I received and the sound of resentment in the woman's voice when she said to watch my bank account around Tabitha.

I asked Tabitha about the phone call as we lay in each other's arms one Saturday afternoon when I lied and told Mike that I was out shopping and needed some alone time.

"Did she say her name?" Tabitha asked with concern.

Stroking the softness of her thigh as it rested upon my own leg, I answered, "No she just cautioned for me to watch my bank account."

Sitting up she pulled the soft sheet around her bare breast, "She called you at work?"

"Yes, Tabitha is there something that I need to be worried about?"

Looking at me with panic in her eyes she said, "That was probably my ex-girlfriend Alexis."

"Is she the one from your birthday party?"

She shook her head yes, "She was becoming very possessive and jealous so when I broke things off with her she got mad. She started calling all of my friends and telling them lies about me. She even called my previous employer and that is how I lost my job."

I sat up wrapping my arms around her trembling body, "Would she try to harm you physically?"

"No, Alexis is all talk, but I'm so sick of her bothering me. Why won't she just let me go?" She sobbed, "She has made my life a living hell."

"Don't worry about it, she will eventually get the point and go away." I reassured her, "We all deal with a crazy ex from time-to-time."

Smiling, Tabitha looked at me and asked, "What is your favorite crazy ex story?"

This was a question that I didn't even have to think about because I never had a crazy ex, "Mike has been my one and only Tabitha."

Skeletons

With her eyes widened she laughed loudly, "Are you kidding me? You have only been with one person your entire life!"

"No I've only been with one man, but I had a lover in college and she was fantastic, but not crazy."

"Aww I'm kind of hurt that I'm not you're first." She pouted. "Does Mike know about this lover?"

"Hell no, I wouldn't dare tell him about this. Mike is a religious fanatic who despises homosexuality in every form."

"Wow what a head job he is. I can't believe that you've only been with one man your entire life though. That is the oddest thing that I've ever heard." She laughed, but I didn't get the joke.

Embarrassed I got out of bed and began putting my skirt on, Tabitha came to me and gave me a hug, "I'm sorry Santana I didn't mean to offend you. It is just that in this day and age I don't see many people who have only been with one person."

"Well it is not like this was intentional," I defended, "It just ended up that way."

"Wow, I can't even get my mind to think what it would be like to have been with only one guy my entire life. Dicks come in so many shapes and sizes and pussy comes in so many flavors. Girl you have been deprived!" she laughed once again.

I didn't see the humor in all of it.

Sensing my irritation Tabitha kissed me softly on my lips down to my collar bone, to my bare breast, shoulders and down to my stomach, "I'm glad to be your second." She smirked before laying me back on the bed and burying her face between my thighs once again.

Mike and the kids were watching a movie when I finally came home that evening, I grabbed a slice of pizza that he ordered and sat on the couch next to Malik. Looking at my life and my family I seemed to have it all, a nice house, two very nice cars, two wonderful children and my high school sweetheart. However, on the outside things can be very deceiving because inside I was unhappy and bored with my life and with my marriage.

That night after ho-hum sex with Mike, he retreated to his side of the bed and I to my own side with no loving words being said.

Shimeka R. McFadden

27
ASTERIA

Picking up my phone I sent Keith a text:
Miss you already
But as usual he didn't respond so that meant that he was either with my sister or some other bitch. At this point it didn't even matter to me because I know that Keith really wants to be with me, but I understand that he has an obligation to my sister as well. Just as we once shared a womb, we now and forever will share a man.
While I was in love with Keith and I wanted him to love me, I didn't see a point in my putting my life on hold for him, so I decided to start taking a few men up on their offers to take me out on a date. I figured since Keith can play the field so should I, after all I am not the one that is married and unlike my sister I refuse to sit at home every night waiting on a man who may never come.
Eric was tall, light and handsome and he had been trying to get me to go on a date with him for months, but because I held out hope for Keith to finally come to his senses I always declined him. Eric was not only handsome, but he also had a good job as part owner and mechanic for an automotive repair shop and most importantly he was single, available and child free. I was excited to finally be able to go out on an actual date rather than sit at home waiting to get fucked night after

night. The life of the mistress isn't an easy one and while I was not ready to let Keith go completely, I was ready to finally enjoy my life and have fun being treated like a lady.

Eric took me to Chipotle Grill he suprised me by being a real gentleman. He not only opened car doors for me, but also he made sure to pull my chair out at the dinner table and allow me to order whatever I wanted from the menu. Keith's idea of taking me out to eat was ordering take out. I knew that he was attractive while in his mechanic's uniform, but Eric also cleaned up very nice making him look even better. Keith better stay on his toes because Eric can give him a run for his money.

"How long have you been living in St. Louis?" I asked after he told me that he was from Florida.

"I have only been here two years off and on." He answered.

"Oh, so you are a virgin." I laughed.

"I guess that you could say that since I've mainly stayed on the coasts. I've lived in Florida, Maine, New York and California."

"Wow so much moving, are you sure that you aren't running from the law Eric?" I joked.

"No, I just feel that since I'm still single with no children I get on my bike and go wherever the wind takes me."

"That is understandable, live your life while you can."

My phone vibrated with a new text alert, but I ignored it.

"Where have you lived?"

"I was living in Phoenix, but when my mom died I came back to St. Louis to be with my twin sister, Pandia, and that is when we decided to open up Gods and Goddess."

"That was nice of you to have left your life down South to come up here to be close to your sister."

"Yeah, I love my sister and we are all that we have. Besides Phoenix was too hot and I can't operate in the heat."

We both laughed, I felt my text alert vibrate again, but I ignored it because I was having such a good time with Eric.

Following dinner he drove me back to my place where I saw that Keith's truck was parked in his usual hiding place and instantly I regretted ever beginning things with him.

"Thanks for dinner Eric, I had a nice time." I said as he walked me to my door.

"Damn, I don't get invited in for sex!" he joked, "Seriously though thank you for allowing me to spend some time with you finally. See it was not all that bad was it?"

Laughing I wanted to invite him inside, but thanks to Keith my night

was ruined, "No it wasn't and I hope that we can do it again."
"And again..." he leaned and kissed me softly on my cheek. "Call me." He whispered in my ear then walked back to his car.
I was floating on cloud nine when I came inside of the house, but my balloon was quickly deflated when I saw Keith lying across my couch.
"How cute." He said sarcastically, "I can actually see you with a mechanic." Ignoring him I went to my bedroom and began undressing, Keith followed behind, "Where Latif?"
"Maybe if you took your ass home sometimes you would have known that he is at your house with Pandia."
"You actually want me to go home?" he laughed, "After all of these years of begging for me to stay, I'm shocked."
"Keith I'm tired and I don't feel like it." I went into my bathroom and washed the makeup off of my face.
When I came back into the bedroom Keith was lying across my bed, naked as usual. "I guess that you don't feel like this either." He said pointing at his erect dick.
With contempt in my eyes and voice I asked, "Is that all this will ever be Keith?"
Holding up his left hand he pointed to his ring finger, the bastard doesn't even bother to take his wedding band off when he came over anymore.
"Well then take your ass home if that ring means that much to you!" I snapped.
Keith walked over to me, putting his strong arms around me, "Don't do this Asteria. You know how I feel about you and I know how you feel about me or are you going to let the mechanic come between us?"
"Eric has nothing to do with the way that I've been feeling Keith. I'm sick of being on standby mode all of the time." I pulled away from him and plopped down on my bed. "You are living a life, but what in the hell am I living?"
"You knew this when we started fucking around..."
"Is that your only defense Keith because I'm sick of hearing it? I am single, but you are married. You made me promises that you knew you weren't going to keep and I am foolish for keep believing you and your bullshit."
"Cut to the chase Asteria because I have to get home soon." He yawned.
Looking at the man that I knew that I would love for the rest of my life I said the words that I didn't think that I would ever say to him, "Keith it is over please leave and don't come back unless it is to see Latif."
Keith's deep voice let out a laugh as he walked towards me, his dick fully erect, he stood in front of me pulling my arms above my head, laying

me down on the bed with the weight of his body on top of me. I could feel his hard, dick on my bare thighs, "It's not over until I say that it is over." Keith spread my thighs with his knee and slid inside of me with force and aggression. "Don't ever tell me no." He growled as he pounded my body and bit my neck. As much as I wanted to push Keith off of me, as much as I wanted to hate him, my heart wouldn't let me and it was my heart that allowed my legs to open wider to him taking him all of the way inside of me.

After he finished, Keith got out of bed and began getting dressed. There were no begs from me asking him to stay because this time I wanted him to leave.

"I don't give a damn that you date Asteria and I sure as hell don't give a damn who you fuck, but if that nigga puts his hand on my child I will kill him then I will kill you." Keith said as he turned and walked out of the bedroom then out of the door heading home to his family.

"How was the date?" Pandia asked when I came into the shop the following Tuesday.

"It was okay." I answered dryly as I tried to avoid eye contact with my sister.

"What do you mean that it was just okay? Girl you have been so tied up with Mr. Mystery Man that you don't even know how to date anymore." Rolling my eyes at her for being stupid and weak for Keith I said, "Yeah, well since you are happily married why don't you tell me how to date sis." I retorted with a hand on my hip.

Pandia was taken aback by my spitefulness and said, "Well excuse me Asteria, had I'd known that this was bring your bitch to work day I would have brought Tweet to the salon." She said about her pit bull.

"Good morning ladies." Keisha said as she walked into the salon.

I cut my eyes that Keisha then walked back to my office, slamming the door behind me. Soon Londyn knocked at the door letting herself in, she had her curly afro pulled back into a pony puff which made her round, chubby face look angelic.

"Talk to me girl." She said matter-of-factly as she sat in the chair in front of my desk. "I have never seen you talk to your sister like that before and there is obviously an issue between you and Keisha so lay it on me."

"There isn't an issue Londyn." I lied.

"Is this about Keith?" she put dryly.

Looking at her in shock I couldn't say anything.

"You didn't think that I knew did you? I may be a lot of things, but the one thing that I am not is a damn fool."

"How did you find out?" I asked trying to hide the fact that my heart was pounding hard in my chest and my breathing was ragged.
Londyn popped her gum and said, "One would be a fool not to have noticed how Keith sits in that girl's chair smiling and carrying on and that hoe just eats it up every chance that she got."
She knew about Keisha, but not about Keith and me, relieved I said, "Yeah I just found out, she is a scandalous bitch Londyn."
"Is that the reason that you were going to fire her?"
"Yes."
"Well why didn't you?"
"Because I felt bad about it and we don't have anyone to fill that booth right now."
"Did that hoe feel bad while she was fucking your sister's husband?" she asked, "And that booth would be filled in no time."
I was silent.
"Any woman that fucks another woman's husband is a disgraceful bitch and should be handled. You and your sister are all that the two of you have so you have to stick up for her in any way that you can." She added. "I know that if a bitch was fucking my sister's husband while smiling in my face, I'd handle her right away." Standing Londyn added, "Get your sister's back Asteria, don't let anyone play her in her face like that."
Once Londyn walked out of my office I felt like an awful person, I knew that what I did was wrong, but at this point I didn't know how to make it right.

Shimeka R. McFadden

28
JOVANNA

BOOM!
The loud sound rang throughout our house waking Justin and I from our sleep.
BOOM!
The sound rang again, it sounded as if someone were trying to kick our door in. Justin jumped out of bed, ran to the closet and grabbed his .45 out of the case.

"Go hide in the closet and dial 9-1-1! He ordered as I looked at him walk slowly into the living room pointing the gun towards whomever or whatever that was trying to enter our home.

Grabbing my cellphone I ran into the closet and dialed the police, as I was talking to the operator I heard three loud shots ring out.

KAP!
KAP!
KAP!

Running out of the closet, I watched in horror as Justin fought with a much larger man over the gun. The man punched Justin in the face sending my future husband slamming into the wall knocking pictures onto the floor shattering them at his bare feet. Justin lunged towards the dark figure throwing his own brand of fury at the agitator's face, landing each punch with precision. People thought that Justin was just a rich white boy, but before Justin's parents came into their money he lived in a bad neighborhood in the Bronx and he didn't mind taking or dishing out an ass whooping and from the sounds of his punches landing he was not playing.

"Jovanna, grab the gun!" he yelled.

I searched around on the floor for the gun as Justin and the perpetrator fought, I found the large weapon underneath the couch and pointed it at the criminal who just landed a punch in Justin's stomach and took one in return.

"STOP OR I WILL SHOOT!" I yelled as I pointed the heavy gun, but the criminal pulled away from Justin and ran back out of our shattered door with Justin following behind, but stumbled down the ten ice-covered stairs that lead to our house. The criminal ran down the street finally getting into a waiting red Cadillac.

"You should have shot him." Justin breathed as he tried to take the gun from my hands, but I gripped the gun tightly. "Babe, let go." He said as he forced the gun from my grasp.

Coming out of my trance I looked at Justin's bruised and swollen face throwing my arms around him, "Baby are you okay?"

"Yeah, I know it looks bad, but I bet that he feels even worse." He said as he wiped the bright red blood that ran down the side of his mouth.

The police arrived five minutes later to take a report, pictures of the damage to the house and to Justin's face. Justin called his brother to take me to a hotel for the night while he and his father fixed the damage to the front door. Still in shock I threw a pair of tattered grey sweatpants and a pink hoodie on. As Sam drove me to the Moonrise Hotel I kept looking behind us to make sure the red Cadillac wasn't trailing us.

"Are you alright Jovanna?" Sam asked.

I knew that Justin's family didn't care about me, but Sam has always treated me fairly, "I'm just in shock." I answered.

"I am too; I can't believe that someone tried breaking into your house while you were there! That is crazy."

Looking in the side mirror I answered, "People these days are crazy Sam. I told Justin that I wanted to get out of St. Louis after we get married. I can't imagine raising children here."

"It isn't all that bad, Mandy and I have been living here for fifteen years and our children are fine. You guys live in a pretty safe neighborhood so maybe this was just some random asshole looking for something to steal so that he can pawn it and get his fix. I bet that he wasn't prepared for what Justin had for him though." He laughed, "The one thing that living in the Bronx has taught us was how to defend ourselves."

Smiling when I thought of how Justin gave it to the criminal I said, "Yeah, I've never seen that side of Justin before and I have to admit I was kind of turned on."

Sam stayed with me while I checked into the hotel room and I got settled.

"Thanks Sam." I forced a smile as I hugged him.

"No problem Jovanna; I know that my family hasn't been the most receptive to you and Justin getting married, but I know my brother and if he loves you then I love you and I don't care what my family thinks. All that I care about is that you treat my brother right."

"Thank you Sam, that means so much." I gushed trying to fight with the tears that were forming in my eyes. It felt good knowing that Sam accepted me and trusted me with Justin's heart, but Sam only knew Jovanna and not who I truly was. If Sam or anyone knew what I was hiding in my closet my life would be over and Justin would never talk to me again.

This had to stop and I had to settle this with Chad once and forever before he got to me first.

29
SANTANA

After pulling Mya's curly hair into a ponytail and wiping the oil off of her forehead I wrapped my daughter in my arms and kissed her soft cheeks.
"I love you.
"I love you too mommy, I love daddy and I love Malik."
"That is so sweet."
"Mommy, do you and daddy still love each other?"
Taken aback by the question I swallowed hard and asked, "Why would you ask that question honey?"
"Because you never kiss anymore and you always fight."
"Honey, married people fight and still love each other."
"Why don't you kiss him anymore?"
"We do kiss Mya."
"No you don't. When I go over to Tanisha's house, her parents always kiss and hug each other and that is because they are still in love, but you and daddy aren't. Are you getting a divorce?"
"Well sometimes grown ups get busy and forget to kiss one another, but that doesn't mean that we are getting a divorce."
"That is what happened to Janelle's parents," she explained, "When her parents stopped kissing they got a divorce because they didn't love

each other anymore."

"That is not going to happen Mya." I said and kissed her on the cheek again.

"But mommy, you didn't answer the question." She looked me in my eyes with innocence.

"What question?"

"Do you still love daddy?"

Trying to swallow the lie that was in my throat I answered, "Your daddy and I will always love each other and we will always love you."

When Mya ran off to play I went into the office to pay bills online, when I viewed my Visa bill I was shocked at the three-thoudand and elevan dollar balance that stared at me from the screen. At first I thought we had been a victim of credit card fraud until I started going over the charges on the account. The dinners, gifts and nights out that Tabitha and I were enjoying were all paid for with my Visa card not to mention the loan that I'd given her to help pay for her past due car payment. I'd never run the credit card bill up to this amount and if Mike found out about it he was going to flip. Quickly I transferred fifteen-hundred from my personal checking into the Visa account bringing the total down slightly, but I still had to make sure that Mike didn't find out about the charges and I had to get the money that I loaned Tabitha back as soon as possible.

"Hey." Mike said when he walked into the office, startling me.

"You scared me." I breathed as I closed the page. "What's up?"

He walked over and sat on the edge of the large wooden desk given to us by his father after we moved into the house, "What are you doing?"

"Paying some bills."

"Would you like to go out tonight after Bible study?"

"That sounds nice, where would you like to go?"

"Mya wants Fritz's Rootbeer and Malik wants Olive Garden again." He sighed.

Disappointed that he wanted to go to dinner with the kids I said, "Not tonight, but you guys go ahead and have fun without me."

"That is what we have been doing." He fumed as he walked out of the room.

I didn't feel like arguing with Mike tonight so I just let him and the kids leave and I called Tabitha when they were in the car.

"Hey sugar!" she yelled over the loud music playing in the background.

"Hey, where are you?" I asked.

Laughing she said, "Out and about, what's going on?"

"I need to talk to you about that loan."

Skeletons

"What; I'm sorry I can barely hear you the music is too loud."
"I said that I need to talk to you about the money that I loaned you for your car payment!" I yelled into the phone.
"I still can't hear you!" she yelled, "Send me a text message because the music is so loud in here."
Then she hung up.
Even though I thought that she heard me, I sent her a text message:
Hey Tabitha I really need to talk to you about that money that I loaned you. Call me as soon as you can.
Fifteen minutes passed when I got the return text:
Let's talk about it tomorrow TTFN!
As soon as I put my cellphone down it rang; it was Asteria and she was frantic.
"Asteria, calm down what is going on?"
"Jovanna and Justin's house was broken into and she is staying at a hotel!"
"Do you know which hotel?"
"The Moonrise."
"How did you find out?" I asked as I slipped on a pair of tennis shoes.
"Keith told me." She answered, "Are you on your way?"
"Yes, I'll meet you there."
I rushed out of the door forgetting all about Tabitha for now because one of my best friends needed me.
When we got to the hotel, Jovanna was hesitant about opening the door until she saw that we weren't going anywhere.
"What is going on?" Asteria exclaimed as she burst through the room, "Keith told me that your house was broken into and Justin was attacked."
Jovanna and I both looked at Asteria funny when she said that Keith told her about the crime, but since he was married to her sister we didn't think much about it.
"I don't know what happened, one minute we were asleep in bed and the next Justin was fighting for his life and I was pointing a gun." She answered as she lowered her small frame onto the bed.
"Did they catch the guy?" I asked with concern.
Jovanna shook her head, "No, but Justin kicked his ass."
"Were you hurt?" Asteria asked rubbing our sobbing friend's back.
Jovanna shook her head, "Justin's face is bruised and battered though."
"Why didn't you call us when this happened?" I asked.
"I didn't want to bother you with my problems."
"We are your friends, closer than sisters and there is no problem that you have that we cannot come together and handle." Asteria fussed,

"There are no secrets between friends."

"Thanks for being here for me." She smiled with a worried look on her face.

"Where is Justin?" I asked.

"He went back to the house last night, but I wanted one more day to myself."

"Are you afraid to go home?" Asteria asked.

"No I just needed some time to think." Jovanna rose from the bed, walked to the mini bar and grabbed a small can of Pepsi.

Asteria and I looked at one another disturbed by her odd behavior.

"You know that you can always stay with Mike and I, we have the guest suite in the basement." I offered.

"And you can always stay at my place, Latif can sleep with me, I just hope that you like The Backyardigans."

Nervous laughter filled the room.

"Thanks guys, but honestly I am going to be fine; Justin is driving me crazy because he is worried about me, so I decided to stay here another night. It has been awhile since I've slept in bed alone and I hate to say it, but it feels good." She laughed.

"Girl tell me about it!" I joined, "I love when Mike's company sends him away for weekend conferences, and I finally get the T.V., the bed and the bathroom all to myself."

"Well I don't have that problem." Asteria said.

"That is because you are wasting your time with Mr. Anonymous." I said. Asteria rolled her eyes.

My text alert chimed it was Mike:

Where are you?

I text back:

At the Moonrise with Jo and Asteria, I will be home in a few.

Mike text back:

Always an excuse.

I ignored his last text message.

"My house was a wreck the last time I was there. Justin said that he and Sam cleaned it up and replaced the front door with security locks and he even went the extra mile and installed a security camera above the front and back doors. I told him that it was unnecessary, but he insisted."

"A real man protects his home." I said.

"I'm just glad that you are alright, hopefully Justin gave that punk a good Bronx-style ass whooping so he will think twice about breaking into someone's house again." Asteria added, "Since you are alright I'm going to let you get some rest."

Skeletons

"Yeah, I have to get home to Mike and the kids, but if you need anything you better call. No more secrets Jovanna." I said as we embraced.
"Okay, thanks guys." Jovanna said as she escorted us to the door.
I couldn't help the feeling that my friend was hiding something from me, but that thought quickly left when my phone rang…it was Tabitha.

Shimeka R. McFadden

30
ASTERIA

Wednesdays were usually our slow days at the salon. So I was stunned when I walked in from having lunch with Santana and Jovanna by the sounds of screaming coming from the salon. Rushing into the salon I saw Pandia wielding a pair of shears in one hand and a hot marcel iron in the other. Londyn was standing next to my sister trying to calm her down, Aaron was holding Keisha back.
"What in the hell is going on?" I yelled.
"This trifling bitch is fucking my husband!" Pandia said as she tried to run towards Keisha, but Londyn grabbed her arm.
"No, your husband was fucking me!" Keisha screamed back.
I quickly grabbed the hot marcel irons out of my sister's hand being careful as not to burn myself with them. "Let's calm down for a moment before someone gets hurt."
Tears of anger streamed down Pandia's face, "Fuck that Asteria, I swear that if I get my hands on that bitch I'm going to jail tonight because she rolling out of here in a body bag."
"I'd like to see you try bitch. You are going to run out of here crying just as you are almost every other week. Shit bitch everyone here knows that Keith has been fucking around on you, but you are stuck on stupid."

Secretly praying that she didn't mention my name, I said to Aaron, "Get her out of here please."

"I don't need anyone to take me out of here, I'm a grown ass woman I'm going to walk out of here with my head held high, too bad I can't say the same for everyone in here though." She said cutting her false eyes in my direction.

"What is that supposed to mean bitch?" Pandia asked. "I hold my head up high every day because he married me bitch! A hoe like you will never have a ring around your finger."

Shaking her head as she put her leather coat on Keisha said, "A ring don't mean a thing because Keith was up in this all of the time and guess what he will be up in this every night after today too. Bitches like you kill me, thinking that because you roped a nigga into marrying you that he won't stop being a man. Please, Keith has been cheating on you for a long time. Trust me I'm not the only one up in this salon that has had a taste of his shit!"

At that point I lost it, "Keisha get the fuck out of here now!" I screamed. Aaron grabbed Keisha by her arm and led her out of the salon as Londyn held my sister back.

It was hard watching the tears stream down my twin's face as we sat in my office and I felt that most of this was my fault. Had I not been afraid of Keisha telling her my secret I would have gotten rid of her before it even came to this.

"I can't believe that bitch Asteria." She sobbed, "She worked with me every day, and she brought her black ass in my salon knowing that she was fucking my husband."

"Calm down sis, she is gone now." I tried to reassure her, but the hurt was too deep for her.

"Scandalous bitch, now I have to go get tested because there is no telling what she has. I wish that you would've fired her ass Asteria."

"I was trying to be fair, but I see what that got me."

"In this world there isn't shit to being fair; fuck being fair because hoes like that will trample all over you as soon as your back is turned. She better hope that I don't run into her on the street because if I do her ass is mine and I don't' give a fuck about going to jail. I have money I can bond out!" Pandia punched the door.

"I didn't know, but Londyn brought it to my attention how Keisha was getting chummy with Keith, but I wouldn't have never thought that she would fuck him and vice versa."

"Londyn knew and she didn't tell me?" Pandia asked in amazement. "I thought that she was my friend."

Skeletons

"It is not like that, Londyn came to me about how Keisha was acting towards Keith and I told her not to say anything to you and let me watch it for myself. I'm sorry but I didn't want to add more stress to your life honey."

My sister sat silently for a few moments, just staring at the picture of mom that was on the side wall. "She was beautiful." She finally said.

Looking at the picture of our mother I smiled, "Yes she was."

"I often wonder if she is proud of us."

"I bet that she is proud of you. You always made her proud, whereas no matter what I did she seemed not to notice or even care." I said wrapping my arms around my sister's body.

"I feel so foolish; how can I face the other stylists after what just happened?"

"Easy, you are going to wipe your tears and walk out there with your head held high and if they don't like it they can quit."

"You are all I have Asteria and I love you." She hugged me tight.

"I love you too." I said in return trying to ignore the sickening feeling of guilt that was building in my stomach.

I invited Eric over for dinner the following night and it was good to see him and to finally have a man who actually wanted to spend time with me instead of just have sex with me on his terms. After dinner I put Latif down for bed then Eric and I sat on the couch enjoying a glass of wine and good conversation.

"So tell me why a lovely, educated and beautiful black woman such as yoursel single?"

"I don't know, I guess that I haven't found the right sexy, accomplished and kind black man to make me his yet."

"Maybe you are looking in all of the wrong places."

"Maybe I have been."

"What is going on with Latif's father, if I may ask?"

Sighing heavily thinking about Keith made me angry and resentful, "He decided to stay with the person that he promised his life to." I answered trying to hide the hurt in my voice.

"I see."

"It was hard, but it was also my fault. I knew better than getting involved with a married man in the first place. But you can't help who your heart falls in love with."

"I have been down that road one too many times myself so trust me I am not one to pass judgment."

"I've learned my lesson and for now on I want my own man, someone who doesn't have to run home to his wife, someone who can take me to dinner and the movies."

Eric sat his glass of wine carefully on the table and looked at me deep in my eyes and said, "And you deserve that." He leaned over covering my lips with his own and kissed me not with lust, but with passion and desire.

In three years Keith has been the only man that I have kissed and in those three years I haven't felt this amount of passion and this is what I've been waiting for.

I ran my hand from his neck down to his chest, while Eric was not as cut as Keith, but his body was solid. From his chest I ran my hand down to his stomach but when I tried to go lower Eric grabbed my hand and stopped me.

"No, no baby I want to take this one step at a time. I want you so bad, but I want to make sure that we won't waste each other's time."

Not knowing what to say I pulled back from him and just stared into his eyes, "Do you like basketball?" was all that I could manage.

Eric laughed, "Yes."

"There is a game on right now; would you like to watch it with me?"

"I thought you'd never ask." He smiled.

Taking him by the hand I led him up to my bedroom where we laid across the bed and watched the game. For the first time in a long time I felt like a girlfriend and not just a bottom bitch.

Tell him to leave NOW

It was 3:30 in the morning and Keith was texting me. Eric and I fell asleep watching the game, we both still had on our clothes. I got out of bed and walked into my bathroom to text Keith back.

No go home to your wife Keith

Keith:

Oh NOW you want me to go home to my wife?

Me:

Things have changed

Keith:

What has changed?

Me:

THINGS now go home I am tired of playing games

Keith:

Who is playing games?

Me:

You said that you were going to leave and that we were going to move to Seattle I was stupid for believing you.

Skeletons

Keith:
We are you just have to give me some time.
Me:
You have wasted enough of my time
Keith:
Where is my son?
Me:
Asleep. Keith go home or to Keisha's house and leave me alone.
Keith:
The mechanic must have given it to you good tonight
Smiling at how immature his mind was always stuck on sex, I text:
No sex involved unlike some who only want me for their own pleasure
Keith:
He is a punk and I should come and kick in your door
Me:
How would you explain that to your wife Keith?
Keith:
You let me handle her
Me:
LOL I have been hearing that for the past three years
Keith:
Tell him to leave so that I can handle you too
Me:
Good night
After hitting send I turned my phone off and got back in bed with Eric and a smile on my face.

31
JOVANNA

"Why have you been so distant lately?" Justin asked as I put lotion on my legs after getting out of the shower.
Irritated by his constant questions I answered, "Justin I have already told you a million times that I haven't been distant now could you quit with the questions."
"I'm sorry but I am just concerned about you. You haven't been yourself lately."
"I just have a lot on my mind."
Justin watched me put on my workout clothes; I told him that I was going out for a run and that I'd be home in an hour. I knew that by the time I made it home Justin would be already gone to work and that is just how I wanted it.
The cold air stung my lungs as I rounded the forth lap of my two mile run, since I'd been so busy planning the wedding and at work I haven't had a lot of time to do what I loved best, running. I needed to run in order to think without constant questions from Justin; all I needed was the sounds of my own breathing, the pounding of my feet on the pavement and Lenny Kravitz blaring through my headphones. Running down Skinker I suddenly felt faint, trying to shake it off I picked up my pace and pounded harder and faster until I rounded the coner of Skinker

onto Lindell suddenly losing my footing and tripped over my own feet, something that I have never done before. Failing at stopping my fall I went down hard, falling face-first on the jagged pavement. I called out in pain as my already cold knee hit the sidewalk; another runner took her headphones out of her ear she slowed her pace enough to ask me if I were alright.

"I'm fine thanks." I breathed with a gloved thumbs up.

I was still on my knees trying to recover the items that fell out of my pockets when I heard the squeak of car breaks and the smell of exhaust fumes behind me. Raising slowly I didn't know if I should run or stay and fight; since it was early morning I knew that other runners were also on this trail so I decided to face him.

"I see that you are still on the run." He smiled showing two gold teeth nestled on his canine teeth. Another man followed closely behind him, wearing the effects of Justin's fury on his swollen eye.

"What do you want Chad?" I asked firmly trying to hide the fear that was nestled in my stomach.

"Now is that any way to treat an old friend?"

"Fuck you!" I spat.

"I told you that she was a fiery one." He said to his associate. "I think that you know what I want."

Two male runners jogged past us looking at Chad strangely.

"Don't worry I will get you your money then after that I want you to disappear as if you were never born."

"You know, I am starting to get use to St. Louis and I was just telling my friend that I think that I may stay awhile." He took a long drag of the cigar blowing it towards my face.

"Do what you will but leave us alone." I fumed as I turned to run away.

"That was a pretty nasty fall that you took, you need to be more careful it can be dangerous for a young lady to be out on these streets by herself these days."

Looking at his friend's swollen eye I said, "No I think that I will be alright." Turning I ran away from him trying to ignore the pain in my knee and the fear in my heart.

Not knowing where I was going to get the ten-thousand dollars that I took from Chad since most of our money was tied up in the lavish wedding we had planned. Even if I maxed out both of my credit cards I would only have seven-thousand of what I needed. Later that evening I searched throughout our modest home looking for anything of value that I could sell to get the rest of themoney that I needed to finally settle things with Chad. Walking around the house I twisted the large

Skeletons

engagement ring on my finger and hated the thought that ran across my mind. Sliding it off of my finger I studied the stunning 18 karat white gold and platinum diamond encrusted ring, the princess cut diamond was flawless. Sam told me that Justin saved up for six months in order to have enough to get me this treasure and I loved it.

I remember when Justin proposed to me as we jogged around Forest Park, stopping briefly in front of the Jewel Box the exact spot that we met three years prior. Justin yelled out in pain as he fell down to the ground holding his calf muscle. I reached down for him only to find him holding out a black ring box with this beautiful ring nestled between the cushions.

"Will you run with me for the rest of our lives?" he asked as I looked on in amazement and shock.

"Yes." the only word that I could utter and the only one that mattered at that moment.

It is hard to believe that six months later I would hand over the ring to a jeweler as I prepared to sell it in order to get Chad out of my life forever.

"Twelve hundred." The old jeweler offered.

"He paid over three-thousand for it."

"Yes and it is beautiful, but I'm only offering you twelve and that is being generous."

Adding the numbers in my head that only gave me eighty-two hundred dollars, still not enough, "Fifteen and I'll throw in this." I offered holding up the white gold Tag Hauer watch that Justin bought for my thirtieth birthday.

"If you say so sweetie." The jeweler said with a smile as he studied the expensive time piece.

I took the rest of the money that we needed from Justin's American Express account, but decided to hold off calling Chad until the queasiness from what I did eased from my stomach.

"I'm sorry about being so pushy this morning." Justin said that evening over dinner.

"That is okay, I'm sorry for being such a bitch." I smiled.

Justin took my hand in his and kissed it noticing that I was not wearing the engagement ring, "Where is your ring?"

I looked down at my plate in shame, "I'd rather not say."

"What do you mean you'd rather not say Jovanna?"

Standing up from the dinner table I limped to the kitchen to grab another bottle of wine from the wine rack. "When I fell I dropped all of my things out of my pocket…"

Justin stood from the table, his face beet red, "You lost your ring!" he exclaimed.
Tears streamed down my face, "I'm sorry Justin, I didn't mean to, but I fell."
"Jovanna no." he yelled. "Do you know how much I paid for that ring?"
I shook my head no, "I tried looking for it, I even had a few of the other runners help me, but we couldn't find it. I think that it landed in the snow."
Justin covered his face in his hands, "I can't believe this."
I cried even harder, "I'm sorry Justin."
He stood up grabbed his leather jacket then walking to the front door. "Where are you going?" I cried.
"I can't deal with this right now. I will be back." He said as he stormed out of the front door.
Hearing the Hemi engine of his truck start up and speed down the street only made the tears come down my face even harder.

Justin didn't return home until well after midnight, I was already in bed when he came in and took off his clothes lying in bed next to me. He smelled like tequila and cigarettes.
"Justin I'm sorry." I whispered.
"It's a good think I got the mother fucker insured." he said before rolling over and going to sleep.
I went to Asteria's shop to get my ends trimmed the next day, I wondered where Keisha was, but Asteria told me not to ask and that she would explain later.
"I can't believe that you lost the ring girl." Londyn said as she clipped my hair, Asteria sat in Keisha's chair as she listened in on the conversation. "I would have been mad too."
"I know but he went a little extreme."
"Girl please you are lucky that he didn't go upside your head." Asteria added, "It is a good thing that he had the sense to get it insured."
"Where did you fall?" Aaron asked as he ear hustled in on the conversation, "I may have to take up running and I need to know the exact location."
We all laughed.
Suddenly Keith walked into the shop, we all fell silent. Pandia cut her eyes sharp enough to slit his throat.
"What do you need?" she asked dryly "There is no one else in here for you to fuck."
Asteria turned her head, "I'm going into my office on that note."
Before she could walk out of the door another gentleman walked in

Skeletons

behind Keith, he was wearing a mechanic's uniform and covered in grease.

"Hey baby, I thought that you might want to get lunch." He said directly to Asteria who looked suprised.

"So you must be the mystery man that we haven't heard enough about." Londyn smiled with her hand on her hip.

Keith eyed the mechanic up and down; if looks could kill the mechanic would have dropped dead on the spot.

"Hi I'm Eric." He said introducing himself to everyone. "You must be Pandia, Asteria has told me a lot about you."

"You work down at Firestone, right?" Keith asked as he sat in Aaron's chair.

"No I own my own shop around the corner on Lindell; I think that we did some work on your F150 not too long ago." Eric answered.

"Oh I forgot."

"Let's go back to my office and talk." Asteria led Eric by the hand into her office and closed the door.

Keith looked as if he could split a brick with his eyes. "It is about time she found someone who would be seen with her in public." He laughed, but none of us though it to be funny.

As I continued my conversation with Londyn about the missing ring I received a text message from Chad:

Tick Tock Tick Tock TIME IS UP bring me my money

Trying to keep this morning's breakfast from building up in my throat I ignored the text and tried to concentrate on the conversation with Londyn.

Justin called as soon as I got into my car; he said that he filed a claim for the lost ring through our homeowner's insurance and that we should hear something back with a week or so. I felt bad for lying to Justin, but I had to make sure that he didn't find out about Chad. Keeping this secret hidden was all that I cared about; Justin would never forgive me if he found out that I was Marquita.

I thought that I was liberated after taking the money from Chad, but I felt even more trapped than what I did before I left. Taking the Greyhound from Memphis to New York then from New York to Ohio and finally ending up in St. Louis. I always had the sinking feeling that I was being followed, so I was nervous to stay put anyplace for too long. When I got into St. Louis the first person that I befriended was Santana, she was pregnant with Mya and had a flat tire outside of the bus station. I helped her change her tire in return she gave me a ride to a hotel dropping me off and handing me her phone number. Santana and Mike were very kind to me, allowing me to stay in their apartment while I finished getting my G.E.D. and working at Pizza Hut. Although Santana was two years older than me, I looked up to her as a mother because she took care of me just like my mother should have.

I didn't meet Asteria until a year later when Santana introduced me to her; Asteria and Santana were best friends from high school. Asteria came home to visit her mother who was recently diagnosed with breast cancer. At that time Asteria was living and working in Phoenix and she would fly to St. Louis every other month to visit her mother and sister as well as hang out with us. We quickly formed a close bond, but there are something's that cannot be shared among friends.

I sent the following text to Chad:

Meet me tomorrow at the Harrah's Casino's iBar no later than 6pm

When I sent the text message the overwhelming feeling of dread came over me and I knew then that I'd made a mistake.

32
SANTANA

Tabitha was sitting at her desk talking on the phone as usual when I called her into my office. We were extra careful not to be seen talking to each other too often because I didn't want to stir up any suspicion that we were fraternizing.
"What's up?" she smiled; I noticed a pair of diamond earrings sparkling in her ears.
"Close the door behind you." I said. Tabitha sat in the chair facing my desk, crossing her legs. Although we'd been together just the other night I longed to nestle my head between the soft folds of her thighs.
"Did you get my text message?" I asked.
"About the money?"
"Yes."
"Yeah, I got it and I'll start paying you off next week when I get paid." She seemed offended.
"Please don't take this the wrong way, but it is just that money is tight at my house and I don't want my husband asking questions about where I spent fifteen hundred dollars."
Rolling her eyes Tabitha flipped her long weave, "I understand; is that all?"
Taken aback by her change in attitude I sat up straight in my chair, "Yes

that is all Tab."
Getting up in a huff Tabitha marched out of my office and didn't speak to me again for the remainder of the day.
I hit traffic on highway 270 on my way so I called Mike to tell him that I would be late and asked if he could start dinner. I zoned out while listening to Ameil Laurreux sing about being free when my cellphone alerted me of a text message from Tabitha:
I need you
I was in between the exit to Tabitha's apartment and my own home and I didn't know which way to go until she sent me another text message this one was a pic of her naked. I text Mike's number:
Send me something to think about while I wait in traffic
Three minutes later Mike sent me a picture of last month's Visa bill that I thought I'd carefully hidden and said:
WE NEED TO TALK ASAP!!!
Needless to say, I turned off on Tabitha's exit.
Tabitha came to the door in nothing more than a smile and the sparkle of the large diamond earrings in her ears. Not hesitating I pressed my lips against hers parting them with my tongue. I was thirsty for her brand of liquor and hungry for her flavor of food. At that moment I wanted Tabitha more than I wanted to go home to my family.
"Slow down baby." She whispered handing me a blue pill, "Let's go to the moon."
I swallowed the tiny pill with a swig of the margarita that she held out for me. "Better yet let's go to Mars." I smiled as I slid out of my pea coat not caring about it dropping to the floor behind me.
"Wait I have something for you." Tabitha teased as she held my hand leading me into the bedroom.
He had to have been made before they broke Adonis' mold because the naked man that lay in Tabitha's bed was a God. At first I was taken aback by his presence, but I was quickly taken in by his body.
"Santana this is Corey." She introduced.
I was speechless as he rose to greet me, his large erect penis leading the way.
"I have heard so much about you." His voice was deep and sensual as he took my hand.
"Corey will be joining us tonight and I hope that you don't mind." She said as she kissed my neck.
The large effects of the tiny pill were beginning to take effect as my entire body began to tingle with every touch that it received from Tabitha and Corey.

Skeletons

At that moment I didn't care anymore; I didn't care about the time, I didn't care about the money, I didn't care about anything except for what was happening to my body at that very moment. Tabitha and Corey took me around the universe and back again and we chronicled it all with pictures that Tabitha took with her iPhone, but I didn't care about that either.

Walking into my house at three-thirty in the morning only to find Mike and the kids gone. There was a single note on the refrigerator that read: *Hebrews 13:4 Marriage is honorable in all, and the bed undefiled but whoremongers and adulterers God will judge.*

I was too tired and sore to deal with Mike and his nonsense so I laid the letter on the table and went to the couch where I slept until it was time for work.

Mike didn't answer any of his calls or texts when I tried reaching him. I tried calling Malik but his phone just went straight to voicemail. It was hard to concentrate at work since I didn't know where Mike had taken the kids. Calling his parent's house, his mother answered, "Hello Santana, how are you?"

"Hi mom, I am fine. Have you seen or heard from Mike and the children today?"

"Yes, they stayed the night over here last night. I don't mean to pry, but is everything alright between you two?"

Breathing a sigh of relief I lied, "Yes mam, we are just having a difference in opinion."

"Submitting to one another in the fear of God. Wives, submit yourselves unto your husbands, as unto the Lord. For the husband is the head of the wife, even as Christ is the head of the church and he is the savior of the body." She quoted from the bible, "All marriages have ups and downs and ins and outs, but remember to seek help from the Lord and everything will work out fine."

"Thank you mom; take care and I will talk to you soon."

"I love you." She said before hanging up.

I was relieved to know that Mike and the children were safe at his parent's home and that he didn't run off and do something crazy.

Tabitha text me during lunch with Asteria:

Corey had fun last night

I text back:

Corey was fun last night lol

"What is going on with you today?" Asteria asked after watching me pick at my salad.

"Mike took the kids and stayed over to his parents' house last night and

I'm not sure of how I should feel."

"You should feel pissed!" she exclaimed.

"I thought that I would be too, but waking up this morning to a quiet, clean house, getting myself ready for work without anyone asking me a million questions I hate to sound mean, but I didn't miss them."

Asteria's eyes widened, "What are you saying?"

"I'm not sure and that is what scares me."

"Wow girl, I didn't know that you two were having problems."

"All marriages have their fair share of issues it is how you handle them that makes a lasting union." I quoted my own mother.

"Have you talked to him?"

I shook my head no, "He won't answer my calls or my texts and I emailed him earlier, but still no answer."

"I am sorry to hear this."

"Don't be; I'm going to give him his space for a few days then we will talk."

"You two have been dealing since high school so if you don't make it then I will question life itself!" she said.

"I think that is half of the problem Asteria." I said sadly, "So how are things with you and the mystery man?" I said changing the subject.

Asteria smiled and fluttered her false lashes, "No more mystery man, his name is Eric and things are going great."

"Wow there is finally a name behind the mystery."

"Yes it feels good to be treated like a girlfriend." She laughed.

"Well I am happy for you."

"Can I ask you a question without being all up in your business?"

"We are friends so you can ask me anything."

"I noticed that you have been spending a lot of time with Tabitha; what is going on with you and her?"

I was extremely uncomfortable with her question, "What do you mean?"

"I am just saying that you two are totally different so when I saw you together at The Melting Pot I was shocked."

"She is my co-worker and she is cool that's all." I tried to hide the truth, "She is young and impressionable so I'm trying to guide her."

"What do you really know about her though Santana?"

Thinking about my friend's question, I really didn't know anything about her at all.

"I'm not trying to be nosey, but I'm just concerned that since you have been hanging with Tabitha things between you and Mike have gone south. If I were you I'd leave the friendship with Tabitha alone and focus more on my marriage."

"How do you know that things between Mike and I haven't already traveled there before Tabitha came into the picture? You really need to stop making half-witted assumptions about someone else's business and focus on your own lonely life." I shot clearly offended.

Looking around for the waiter so that I could pay the bill and hightail it out of the restaurant I continued, "What do you know about relationships anyway Asteria, when for the past three years you have been dealing with a man who won't even acknowledge you in public."

My friend's skin turned red and I could see the fire building up inside of her, "How dare you come at me like that Santana! You think that you are high and mighty because you are married and I am not!"

"No I find it rather strange that you have a baby by a man that we have never met before and that you have allowed yourself to be the bottom bitch for over three years yet you think that you can give me advice." I slammed twenty-five dollars on the table, "How about this, when you stop being a sperm depository for someone else's husband then you can offer me advise!"

Tears welled up in my best friend's eyes as she blinked fast trying to keep them from falling, but they made a fast trail down her soft cheeks. I was embarrassed by the scene that I'd just made and how I felt like a fool. Instead of apologizing to my friend I stood up and walked out of the restaurant as fast as my legs could carry me leaving Asteria sitting there with her mouth hanging open.

The house was quiet when I got home from work; Mike and the kids were staying another night with his parents. I no longer cared about salvaging this relationship; I was tired of bending and flexing to meet the needs of other people while my own needs went unmet. After getting out of the shower, I lay across the sectional in the family room and swallowed one of the tiny pills that Tabitha gave me and closed my eyes trying to forget the life that I worked so hard to build, but worked even harder at tearing apart.

Shimeka R. McFadden

33
ASTERIA

"Santana is lucky that she is my best friend or I would have mopped the floor with her ass!" I fumed as I paced the floor in my apartment that night. Pandia sat on the couch while our sons play together.
"Calm down Asteria, she is just going through some things right now. Give her some space and time and she will apologize." She assured me.
"I don't care what she is going through, that is no reason to treat me like shit!"
Pandia didn't like cursing around little Keith so she shot me a stern look, "Calm down, you are scaring the boys."
I plopped down on the couch next to my sister and laid my head on her shoulder.
After a short silence she asked, "Have you ever noticed how much our son's look like one another?" she said as she watched the boys closely. "See how little Keith has those deep set eyes and long eyelashes now look at Latif, he has the same. Also look at the shape of their nose, exactly the same."
"Well we are twins Pandia." I managed through the knot in my throat.
"But little Keith looks nothing like me, he looks exactly like his daddy."
"Girl please that boy is a spitting image of you and Keith. What are you

trying to say that Latif is Keith's son?" I laughed nervously; I was relieved when her cellphone rang.

"It is Keith." She rolled her eyes, "Hello?"

I sat and listened while my sister talked on the phone to my ex-lover and her headache. Ordinarily I would have been mad, but today I didn't care because the more time that I spent with Eric the less time I desired to spend with Keith.

"Girl I have to go Keith is tripping again." She began packing up their things.

"He has some nerve as much as he stays out at night." I said as I helped her.

"He has some nerve after what happened with Keisha."

"Yeah, I'm still in shock over that."

"Of all people why did he choose that ghetto queen Asteria? Am I not good enough for him?"

"It is not about you Pandia, it is about him. Keith is a selfish son-of-a-bitch who was more concerned about his dick than he is about his marriage. Don't blame yourself for what he did wrong."

"I cook for him, I keep a clean house, and I get freaky in the bedroom…"

"Whoa, wait a minute now, I love you girl but I don't want to hear about your freaky side!" I joked tossing a teddy bear at her.

Pandia laughed, "I'm serious though, what am I doing wrong?"

The hurt in my sister's eyes spoke volumes to me, while I regretted ever laying eyes on Keith I knew that there was no way I could let her know about us. "Again honey, it is not about you it is about him. He is selfish, you could be the perfect wife, flawless mother and the impeccable lover but it will never be enough for someone who is as egotistical as Keith."

"Do you think that he will ever change?"

"Eventually, but how long do you have to wait?" I asked. "I know some women who have been waiting on a man to change for over ten, fifteen or maybe even twenty years Pandia. Do you have a decade to wait around on him to change? Is it fair that he gets to run around living the life of a single man while you still live the life of a married woman?"

Pandia was silent for a moment as we gathered her son's items, "He says that he is stressed at work because of all of the budget cuts, he doesn't know if he will get enough hours or even have a job when he comes to work then when he comes home he gets stressed by all of the responsibility that I lay on him with the house and little Keith."

I couldn't believe the words that were coming from my sister's mouth, "That is a bunch of bullshit Panida! If he is that stressed then he needs to depend upon his wife for comfort not run to the arms of another woman!"

"I know Asteria, but I want my family to work. We grew up without a father and you know how hard that was on momma."

Remembering when my father walked out on us for another woman and never visiting or calling us again really hurt me, but seeing how strong mom was throughout made me proud once again. "Yes it was hard on mom, but she kept her self-respect and we turned out perfectly fine. Besides, you will find another man if that is what you are worried about."

"I don't want another man; I want the father of my child, my husband, at home. That is what is best for little Keith. Being married is so much more complex than you realize Asteria, but if things with you and Eric keep going as well as they have been I'm sure that you will find out how hard marriage is soon."

Ignoring her last comment I helped my sister and her son put on their coats, kissed them both goodbye and walked her to my door. I don't care how complex marriage is, I would never put up with a man cheating on me.

I don't know why I was suprised when Keith walked in an hour after Pandia and little Keith walked out; I felt him climb into bed with me and our son, kissing me softly on my neck.

"What are you doing here?" I whispered.

"I came to see you, but I had to make sure that she was at home."

"You need to leave and go home Keith." I said as I pushed his hand off of my breast.

"Come on now, you have been playing me off for the past week." Keith pulled my tank top down forcefully, ripping it and exposing my bare breast. I jumped up out of bed.

"Keith leave now; it is over between us! I cannot do this anymore. I cannot live with myself knowing what I am doing to my sister."

"Here you go with this bullshit again." He grabbed me by my arm and pulled me to him, "You know that you want this."

Just then Latif started to stir.

"Leave before you wake Latif up."

"I guess that mechanic got your nose wide open now."

"This has nothing to do with Eric, but it has everything to do with me."

"It is funny how you didn't give a fuck about me fucking around on your sister, but now you want to act all holy and shit." Keith fumed, "You better hope that she never finds out about us and the truth about your son."

Folding my arms across my chest I said, "No you better hope that she never finds out."

Keith laughed, "I have nothing to worry about because she will never leave me, but you, well you are her sister and she will never forgive you." Keith yanked my panties down and began toying with my pussy, but I didn't respond to his touch; that didn't matter to Keith he took what he came for then left when he was done.

I didn't move until I heard his truck speed down the street. I knew that Keith would never tell her, but just the thought of what I did made me sick. I couldn't believe that I was a person who would betray the love and trust between twin sisters for a man. Keith was not worth it and if I could turn back the hands of time I would never have slept with him. How could I have been so stupid thinking that he would ever leave his wife for me when deep down I knew that Keith had no intentions on leaving her? I was the selfish one, constantly feeling as if Pandia and I were in some sort of competition when we weren't. The tears stung when they ran down my face, because of my own insecurities I hurt my sister, and ruining her family and now I have to deal with the reality that I may have to raise Latif without his father and spend the rest of my life without my sister.

34
JOVANNA

I'd been fighting an uneasy feeling in the pit of my stomach since I woke up this morning, but I agreed to let Justin take me to lunch where he once again began questioning me about what happened to the ring. I hated lying to Justin, but it was necessary because the truth would hurt him even more. During lunch Asteria called to tell me about her falling out with Santana and to gush about Eric.

Later that evening while Justin was watching the game, I lied and told him that I was going to Santana's house to try to defuse the bomb between her and Asteria, but I was really going to meet Chad and pay him back his money. I put the large envelope that was stuffed with money in my purse and headed out of the door and across the bridge into St. Charles to the casino. I fought the urge to turn and run away as I walked slowly into the casino.

I purposely sat facing the entrance to the iBar so that I could see when Chad entered the room which he did at exactly six o'clock. Dressed in a pair of copper slacks, black and copper cashmere sweater and a fedora. He was alone.

"I am suprised that you showed up." He said as he slid into the seat to my right. "I was prepared to make a visit to your house and talk to your man."

"I knew that you would." I retorted as I grabbed the heavy envelope out of my purse.

"Wow, you move quickly; I thought that we would catch up and reminisce about old times."

"This is what you came for right?" I said handing him the envelope, "So take it and leave me the fuck alone."

With well-manicured hands Chad took the envelop out of my hands and put it in his pocket, "That is easier said than done Marquita." He grabbed my wrist, "You see in my line of work a reputation means everything. A pimp with a reputation of keeping his hoes in their place while keeping his business tight means a lot, but a pimp who lets his hoes walk away with his money isn't shit. What you did to me cost me a lot more than ten-thousand Marquita and that I can't get back."

I swallowed hard, "Let me go or I will scream."

"And if you scream I will make sure your little snowflake and everyone else know exactly who you are and what you are capable of." His southern voice was thick and deep, "Now what you are going to do is walk calmly out of this fine establishment without any fuss."

"Do what you will, but I am not leaving here with you." I spat trying to release my arm from Chad's grasp.

"I wonder how Justin would feel about knowing the woman of his dreams isn't anything more than a two-bit hoe that had bad cocaine habit."

"I am not that person anymore."

"You can't run away from what you truly are. I wonder how many lies you told to get this money that you just handed me. I wonder who you stole it from. How would his family feel about knowing the woman their son was about to marry was a whore? I know that his family is very important in this town, I don't think that they would take too kindly about scandal in their family."

I held my head down low, "Chad what do you want from me? Haven't you taken enough?"

"Get up and let's go."

I knew that he wouldn't stop unless I did what he wanted so I got up and followed him to the parking lot, but I knew that if I got in his car I would never see Justin again. Chad had a tight grasp on my left arm he pushed the button to unlock his car door but as he attempted to force me into the car I reached down and grabbed his nuts with as much force as I possibly could, Chad let go of my arm and bent down in agony. I struggled to get past him and run away, but he reached up and smacked me across the mouth I felt my lip rip open and blood pour out of my mouth. The smack came with so much force that it knocked me back against a black truck that was parked alongside of his Cadillac, instead of falling I regained my balance quickly as I used my heavy purse as a weapon and began swinging it forcefully in his direction, hitting him twice in his head.

Chad grabbed the purse and tried to use it as leverage to pull me closer to him, but I let it go as I tried to run, but I ended up slamming into the truck's side view mirror which sent a different kind of pain through my arm and chest. Chad reached and grabbed me behind my neck, throwing me down to the ground hitting my head on the hard concrete. I attempted to scream, but Chad had a tight grasp around my neck. I could feel my breath being choked out of me as I struggled to keep my consciousness; I flailed my arms in an attempt to fight him off of me. I didn't want to die laying on a cold, hard parking lot in between two cars, I didn't let Chad kill me when I was Marquita and I wasn't going to let him kill me as Jovanna. Gathering all of my strength I reached up with both arms and began clawing at his face and eyes. I dug deep until he released his grasp around my throat. Chad screamed out in pain holding his bleeding with his hands.

"You fucking bitch!"

Coughing I managed to rise to my feet as I staggered away from the cars I saw two women getting out of their own cars and I waved my arms in the air in an attempt to get their attention.

"Help!" I screamed while holding my throat, the women came rushing towards me with concern in their eyes but that concern turned to fear. Suddenly the pain in my back was so intense that it took the remainder of my breath away. I felt the effect before I heard the cause.

I felt as if I were falling in slow motion, I could see the women running towards me and the faint sound of Chad's car starting up then speeding out of the parking lot. Hitting the ground with a thud I felt as if I were paralyzed. But the sharp sting in my back told me that I still had some sort of feeling as the blood trickled down my body onto the stony pavement.

"Hang on honey help is on the way." One of the women cried as she took off her coat and laid it on top of me. I could hear her friend on the phone with the police and three men rushed over to see what was going on.

"Oh my God what happened?" one of the men said as he lifted my head and placed his rolled up coat underneath.

"I don't know someone shot her." The answered.

"Did anyone see who did this?" someone asked.

"No, but we did see a red car with out of state plates drive off."

"Hang on sweetie." The woman said as she held onto my hand, "The police are coming."
I attempted to speak, but agony and weakness made it impossible. I was grateful for all of their help, but I wondered how many of them would have been by my side had they'd known that I deceived my soon-to-be husband and that the man that shot me was my ex-pimp because I stole money from him when I was a prositute.

35
SANTANA

"This is so good." Tabitha smiled as she forked more spaghetti in her already full mouth, "I can't believe that I've never been here before."

I felt bad about pressing her for the money and since Mike wasn't answering his phone, I decided to take her to Maggiano's Italian restaurant. "I can't believe that no one has taken you here either. Mike and I use to come here a lot when we got married."

"Wow it must be nice to have someone splurge money on you like that." I took a sip of my Pinot Noir, "I never looked at it like that. Well someone is spending money on you; look at those rocks you've been sporting in your ears lately."

Tabitha touched the large diamonds in her ear nervously, "I've had these for a while."

"Maybe you should've pawned those to pay your car note."

Tabitha looked insulted, "If you only brought me here to chastise me about the money then you may as well take me back home."

"I'm sorry Tab; I didn't mean to offend you. Let's enjoy the rest of our night together."

"You made me feel bad." She pouted.

"Well maybe later I can make it up to you by making you feel good."

Tabitha raised a perfectly arched eyebrow, "I like how that sounds."
My phone alerted me to a text, to my surprise it was from Mike:
Where are you?
I didn't feel like arguing with him and I was enjoying my night with Tabitha so I ignored the text.
"Has he came back home yet?"
I shook my head no, "Now ask me if I miss him." I winked.
Tabitha laughed I felt her foot on my lap inching its way between my thighs where she used her toes to toy with my pussy. Closing my eyes I smiled, I was transported back to reality when my phone began to ring. It was Mike, if it weren't for the fact that I wanted to make sure the kids were okay I would not have answered.
"Hello?" I answered with annoyance.
"Did you get my text?" he sounded frantic
"Did you get mine from today and yesterday?"
"I don't have time for this Santana; where are you there has been an accident."
My heart sat in my throat, "An accident, are the kids okay?"
"Yes the kids are fine, but Jovanna has been shot."
"Shot what do you mean shot?" My hand trembled as I tried to keep a tight grip on the phone.
"I don't know what happened, but I just got the call from Asteria she said that she tried to call you but you wouldn't answer her calls either."
After our argument the other day I'd been avoiding Asteria's calls.
"What hospital did they take her to?"
"Right now she is at DePaul in the trauma center, but Justin said that they were going to rush her to St. Johns so he is telling everyone to meet there."
"Oh my God Mike, I am on my way." I cried.
Tabitha looked uncomfortable by my crying, "What is going on?"
"My best friend has been shot." I beckoned for the waiter to bring me the check.
"Is she going to be alright?"
"I don't know." I looked through my wallet for my credit card. "Can you get the car from valet while I pay for dinner please?"
"Here, give me your credit card, I'll pay for dinner and you get the car from valet." She snatched the company credit card from my hand, but I was too upset and hurried to even care.
"Are you going to take me home before you go to the hospital?" she asked with annoyance.
"No I don't have time, besides I really need you right now."

Skeletons

I didn't see Tabitha roll her eyes as she looked out of my car window. I drove like a bat out of hell down the highway towards the hospital; Tabitha didn't say a word during the drive. When we got to St. Johns hospital we were told to wait in the emergency trauma center where I saw Mike who was holding a crying Asteria. Mike's eyes went from me to Tabitha then back to me again.

"How is she?" I asked.

Asteria wiped her tears with the back of her hand which smeared makeup across her face and on her hand. "We are not sure yet. Justin just went back to see her before surgery."

I sat down next to my friend and hugged her, "Let's pray that she will be alright."

"That is what we've been doing." Asteria said, "Why wouldn't you answer your phone?"

Ashamed by my behavior I looked down at my clenched hands then over to Tabitha who sat next to my husband. "I was still upset."

"I don't give a damn about you being upset Santana we have been friends since high school and have fallen out countless numbers of times that is still no excuse for you to treat me like this."

"I apologize, but I didn't know that Jovanna was hurt."

Asteria looked at Tabitha, "Why are you here?"

"Excuse me?" Tabitha snapped.

"You heard me why are you here?" Asteria's voice got louder, "Don't think I don't know who you are and what you are about! You may have Santana in your back pocket, but I'm cut from a different type of cloth." My friend fussed with one finger pointed into Tabitha's face.

"Hey let's calm down for a moment." Mike quieted Asteria, "Our friend is hurt so instead of allowing negative energy fuel this moment let's get past our feelings and seek God for help and forgiveness."

Asteria cut her eyes at Tabitha, "Yeah you are right Mike lets pray before I lose my religion."

We bowed our heads and held hands in prayer; I felt comfort in Mike's words and holding his strong hand made me feel even more secure. I knew that Mike loved me, but I didn't know if I wanted to continue to pretend that I loved him the same.

An hour passed before Justin walked out of the back looking tired and distraught. I embraced him tightly as he cried into my arms.

"How is she Justin?"

"I don't know yet, she is still in surgery." He cried, "I couldn't sit back there any longer."

"I am sorry Justin." I said.

Looking at me with tear-filled blue eyes and he said, "I thought that she was with you."

"I hadn't heard from Jovanna since the other day."

"I knew that she'd been lying to me all of this time. First it was the late night phone calls, then she started becoming distant, she lost her engagement ring and now this."

I looked at Tabitha who was cleaning her nails while flirting on her cell phone; I see that I was not the only one who was keeping secrets.

"Had Jovanna confessed anything to you guys about what was going on with her?" he asked.

"No, as far as I knew she was just pre-occupied with your wedding." Asteria said.

"That is what I thought then she told me that she lost her ring when she fell while running which I know is a lie. Jovanna never takes her ring off so why would she take it off just to run? It just doesn't add up."

"It kills me to think that she was living a double life." Justin sighed.

"I know how you must feel; in a marriage there should be no secrets." Mike said while looking directly at me.

Justin sighed, "I wanted to come back here to let you know how she was doing. You are free to go home and I will call you with any updates."

"I am staying right here until I know that Jovanna is going to be okay." Asteria said.

"Me too." I said looking over at Tabitha who was sure to have a fit once I told her about my plans.

"Thanks guys, Jovanna always said that if she didn't have anyone she knew that she would have you." Justin smiled then walked out of the waiting room.

Walking over to Tabitha, who quickly ended her phone call. "So what are we doing?" she asked with irritation in her voice.

"What do you mean?" I asked also irritated by her behavior.

"Are you ready to go home and finish our date.

"No, I'm going to stay here until she comes out of surgery." I said.

"Why would we sit here while she is in surgery when it could take hours? There are plenty of other things that we could be doing besides can't they just call you if anything changes?"

I couldn't believe what my ears were hearing, "Look Tabitha, if you don't want to stay then feel free to go." I fussed in a whisper.

"It is not that I don't want to stay but I just don't see the point. We could just come back after she wakes up from surgery." She pouted.

"And what if she doesn't wake up?"

Tabitha just sighed folding her arms in front of her chest in a huff; I could see Mike eyeing us from across the room.

The time passed slowly without any word from Justin, Tabitha was back on her cell phone and Asteria had fallen asleep.

"Hey I'm going down to the cafeteria to get something to snack on; do you want anything?" Mike asked.

I looked at Tabitha who just rolled her eyes then decided to join him.

"Is that Tabitha?" he asked.

"Yes, she is my assistant."

He hit the down button to the elevator, "Is that all that she is?"

"What is that supposed to mean?"

"I mean you have been spending a lot of time with your assistant lately so I'm wondering if that is all she is to you or is she also a friend."

"I guess that you could consider her to be my friend Mike."

"I am suprised that a girl like that actually works for a living." He added, "She looks as if she is accustomed to being kept."

"Looks can be deceiving. Tabitha is actually a great assistant."

We rode down to the cafeteria in an uncomfortable silence. Mike smelled like Irish Spring soap, I chuckled because that is the only soap his mother and father would use no matter how badly it dried their skin. I remembered our first date all that I could smell was Irish Spring.

"What is so funny?" he asked once we stepped off of the elevator.

"Nothing. How are the kids?"

"They are fine; I told them that you needed some space so we had to stay at my parents' house for a few days. You know that was not good enough answer for Mya, she questioned me for an hour before she was satisfied. Malik was cool because he has his eye on this little girl across the street." Mike explained with a smile. Mike may have sucked as a passionate husband, but I couldn't deny the fact that he was a great father.

"Wow this place brings back so many memories." Mike said as he grabbed a tray. "I remember coming down here to shovel food down my mouth while you were in labor with Mya."

"That girl caused me so much grief." I smiled.

"You were in labor for two days only for her to just pop out after two pushes."

"When the doctors said that she was a girl, the look on your face was priceless."

"I can't believe you and my mother played me like that. You both knew the sex of the baby all along, but you wouldn't tell me."

"I'm sorry, but I knew how badly you wanted a girl and I didn't want to ruin the surprise for you."

"I almost fainted."

"I know!"

We shared a laugh off of our memories.

"What happened to us Santana?" he asked looking deep into my eyes.

I thought about his question for a moment and answered, "We just got bored."

"I was never bored."

"You'd rather watch T.V. than make love to me."

"Is that what this all is about?"

"I don't know what this is all about Mike." I sighed then I got a text from Tabitha saying that she was leaving in a cab.

"Is it another man?" he asked.

"No, it's us." I answered as I looked through my purse trying to find my credit card, but remembered that I'd given it to Tabitha to pay for dinner. Mike handed the cashier his card instead, "I got this by the looks of your Visa bill you can't afford to treat me to a snack."

I rolled my eyes, "I already took care of the bill Mike. Don't worry about it."

"Okay, I can't and I will not live with uncertainty Santana. I can't live with the fact that I don't know how you feel about our marriage and that you are hiding something from me."

"And I can't live with the fact that you can't trust me. I can't live with the fact that you ignore me as if I'm not even there!" I huffed, "Mike this is neither the time nor the place."

"When is it ever the time Santana? You spend so much time running away from our issues that we never get anything resolved."

"I run away because I don't want to face the fact that you are no longer in love with me."

"I never fell out of love with you; you pushed me away."

"Why did you allow yourself to be pushed?" I asked looking my husband in his beautiful eyes. "Why won't you fight for me?"

"Why should I have to fight for someone who suppose to love me in the first place?"

Just then my phone rang it was Asteria telling me that our friend was out of surgery.

36
ASTERIA

Eric suprised me by showing up at the hospital when he heard about what happened to Jovanna; needless to say Keith would have never shown that kind of concern.
"How are you holding up?" he asked as we embraced.
"I am holding up just fine, thanks for coming."
"Does anyone know exactly what happened?"
I shook my head, "The police just said that she was shot in the parking lot of Harrah's and they would have to wait until she wakes up for questioning."
"Is there anything that I can do?"
"Just be here." I answered hugging him tighter.
"Don't worry I will always be here for you."
The doctors said that the bullet missed her spinal cord by two inches and that Jovanna was lucky that she didn't lose the ability to walk. They were able to retrieve the fragments inside of her body, but she would be out of commission for weeks as she recovered and that she may have a lifetime of pain. The doctor suggested that we come back tomorrow after she'd rested from the surgery. Mike and Santana left right after hearing that Jovanna would be alright. Eric and I left an hour later so that we could get some rest. I was hurt that Santana didn't talk to me,

but I figured that it had a lot to do with Tabitha.

Eric and I got back to my house and relieved my neighbor from babysitting Latif.

"Do you mind if I take a quick shower to wash this hospital smell off of my body?" I asked.

"No go right ahead." Eric yawned as he made himself comfortable on my bed.

Stepping into the shower I let the hot water run down me, easing away the tension that was in my neck, arm and back muscles. It had been a long hard week and I just wanted to wash it all away and let it flow down the drain losing it all in the sewers of St. Louis.

Eric stepped inside of the shower, wrapping his strong arms around me. "I have dirt that needs to be washed off too." He whispered in my ear.

I turned facing him staring into his eyes, trying to get lost in them. "Are you real?" I asked.

Smiling Eric pressed his lips against my own; his kiss was filled with desire. "Does that seem real enough to you?"

Eric took the vanilla scented soap pouring it into his right hand and rubbing it on my back and neck until it worked up a thick, rich lather. He then ran his and down my thighs one by one, massaging them intentionally taking his time on each and every inch; down to my toes.

As the sounds of the hot water hitting my body took over my ears, the smell of the vanilla acquired my nose, the taste of Eric's soft lips and moist tongue seized my tastes and the touch of his thick, pulsating dick as it rubbed against my back tempting my skin.

"I want you Asteria, but I only want to take you if you promise me that this is more than just sex. I'm too old to involve myself in a relationship that is built around sex."

Giving him my thirsty tongue only to come up for air to say, "If that is all that I wanted I would have gotten that a long time ago." I smiled.

Eric aggressively pressed my bare breast against the warm, steam-covered glass shower door lifting one leg around the bend of his arm he entered me like a thirsty man drinking from a cup of cold water. I gasped at the force in which he took me, but it wasn't disrespectful and hurried as it had been with Keith. Eric took his time with me, leading me to the bed and making love to every inch of my body; speaking to me softly, making love to every inch of my mind. And with each thrust he made me forget about the hurt, anguish and despair that kept me running back to Keith.

Making love to Eric was the fantastic, but waking up in the morning seeing him still there felt even better. I felt as if we were a family as we made breakfast together while Latif sat at the table coloring. Eric wrapped his arms around me and kissed me on the cheek while I scrambled the eggs and we talked about traveling together while we ate. He left for work and promised that he'd be back tonight; unlike Keith who never promised to return.

"Someone must've gotten them some this morning." Londyn joked when I walked into the salon smiling from ear to ear.
"That would be none of your business." I winked.
Aaron came up and hugged me, "I am so happy that you finally got you some girl. I got tired of seeing you coming up in here looking like a sour puss."
"Speaking of sourpusses," Londyn whispered, "I think that Keith is up to his usual ways."
I looked outside to see Pandia sitting on the patio smoking a cigarette; she looked as if she'd lost her best friend."
"When will she learn?" Aaron said. "Keith is sexy, but damn he isn't sexy enough to put up with all of that. Hell Pandia already looks homely, but give her a few more years she is going to be downright haggard!"
"Let me go talk to her." I sighed heavily.
"How is Jovanna? We heard what happened." Londyn asked with concern.
"She is going to be in the hospital for awhile, but the doctors think that she will be fine."
"Have you talked to her?" Aaron asked.
"No, she was still asleep when I called this morning. Eric and I are going to visit her tonight." I answered as I walked outside to my sister.
"Girl it is too cold to be sitting out here." I fussed as I tightened the belt around my coat. "What is going on?"
Pandia took a long drag from her cigarette, "How is Jovanna?" her eyes were swollen and bloodshot while her voice was light, distant and weak.
"She is going to be fine, but my question is how are you?"
She sucked her teeth, "I went through some of Keith's check stubs so that we could refinance our house next month."
"Okay and…"
"And apparently this mother fucker has another child that he has been paying child support for." She held up the check stub for me to see what I already knew. "Four hundred and fifty dollars a month."
I swallowed hard, "That is crazy Pandia."
"That is why he has been working all of that overtime to compensate what his lousy ass has been paying child support for some bastard child

of his!"

It hurt me to hear her say that about my son, but I knew that it was the truth no matter how much I didn't like it. "It isn't the child's fault Pandia. Stop blaming other people for what Keith does."

"Fuck that bastard kid." She spit, "I hope that bitch that had the baby by him knows that he has herpes"

Blinking hard was all that I could do to keep myself from going off, "Herpes?"

"Yes herpes Asteria; Keith has it and he gave it to me some time ago. Why else do you think that I've been staying with him through all of the bullshit that he has put me through? Thanks to his lousy ass I have a lifetime disease so who is going to want me now?"

I couldn't breathe, herpes, does that mean that I have it as well and I that could have given it to Eric.

Pandia put the cigarette on the ground and stomped it, "I can't wait to see him."

Me either, I thought.

I called my gynecologist as soon as I got into my office and she agreed to see me within the hour. Dr. Franklin was an old family friend and the first to discover the lump in my mom's breast before she was diagnosed with cancer. The checkup was painless and it revealed that I didn't have anything to worry about which was a relief.

Pandia looked at me crazy when I got back to the office after the appointment. I lied and told her that I had to make some deposits at the bank when she asked where I'd been. I felt bad that my sister had herpes but I still felt that it was her own fault for staying with Keith even though she knew that he was cheating on her. I blamed her for being dumb and staying with a man who slept around on her.

I knew that I was wrong for sleeping with her husband, but she was wrong for staying with him and putting not only her heart, but also her body in jeopardy. As much as the sound of his voice made me sick, I had to call Keith and ask him how he planned on dealing with the fact that Pandia knew about the child support that was being deducted from his check.

"What do you mean what am I going to do? I am going to tell her the truth."

"What!" I exclaimed.

"I am going to tell her that I got some chick knocked up and the girl refused to get an abortion."

"What if she wants to see the baby?" I questioned.

"If she wants to see the baby then I am going to tell her that the bitch

moved out of town and that I've never even see the baby."
I sighed, relieved, "You are real trifling Keith; now my sister has to live with herpes for the rest of her life because you just can't keep your slimy dick in your pants."
"Herpes, what are you talking about?" He scoffed.
"Don't play stupid Keith; Pandia told me that you gave her herpes and that you told her that you got it from one of your trifling whores that you have been with."
Keith laughed, "Your sister is using a lie to get the truth." He laughed again, "I've always told her that she should have went to the police academy instead of me. Look I don't have herpes, Pandia doesn't have herpes. I used protection with everyone except you."
Why would Pandia lie to me, I thought then I began to panic; Keith was right, Pandia was using a lie to get the truth.
"I have to go." I said as I rushed him off of the phone.
I knew that it would happen sooner or later, I knew that I couldn't keep my secret locked away in a closet forever. Slowly my skeleton was about to show her ugly head.

Shimeka R. McFadden

37
JOVANNA

The pain that radiated throughout my body woke me up; I looked to my left to see Justin talking to his brother Sam only rushing to my side when he saw that I was awake.

"Jovanna!" he kissed me on my forehead. "Baby are you okay?"

I coughed; it hurt to try to talk.

"Don't say anything save your strength."

"Hey kid, how are you?"

I gave Sam weak thumbs up.

"I am going to go get the nurse to let her know that you are awake." Sam said.

Justin kissed me all over my face; it felt like I'd been in the ring with Floyd Mayweather. Fighting through the pain I reached up and touched the right side of my face which was swollen down to my lips. My neck was so tender and swollen that I could still feel exactly where Chad's hands were gripping it. A single tear ran down my face when I saw the look of hurt on Justin's face.

"What happened sweetheart?" he asked, "Why did you lie to me?"

I shook my head.

"Please Jovanna; please don't lie to me any longer." He begged, "Whatever it is I'm sure that we could work through it, but I cannot take the lies."

Justin put his head down on the bed and sobbed; my heart was in more pain than my body because as much as I wanted to tell Justin the truth, I knew that he would never understand. I had to lie to protect him. Three nurses walked into the room and asked Justin to step out while she checked my wound, my vitals and cleaned me up. I was relieved to see him go because I couldn't stand seeing him hurt so much any longer.

The police came to take a statement from me, but I lied and told them that I didn't know who did this to me and that I didn't see his face. I told them that I was attacked in the parking lot when I was coming out of the casino. After they took my statement Justin came back into the room carrying a large bouquet of roses and a big white teddy bear. Kissing me on the cheek he asked how I was doing.

"I am fine." I managed as I winced from the pain.

"Your friends came when you were back in surgery."

I smiled.

"They really love you."

"I know." I whispered, "I see that you went to the gift shop." I said looking at the teddy bear.

"I know how much you like stuffed animals. Jovanna, why were you at Harrah's that night? Why did you lie about going with Santana?"

I didn't have words to say to him, but when I looked at the amount of worry in his blue eyes I started to cry.

Justin took my hand in his and said, "Jovanna, my mother struggled with a gambling addiction that fueled her alcohol abuse but we got her through it so I know that I can help you get through this."

"A gambling addiction?" I wondered to myself.

"I know the signs, missing jewelry and your maxed out credit card. At first I thought that you were having an affair, but when they said that you were found at Harrah's Casino it began to make sense to me."

The tears flowed down my face even harder.

"It is okay we are going to get through this because I love you, but Jovanna I cannot take you keeping secrets from me any longer. I need you to promise me that the lies and the secrets are over."

Chad had his money and was most likely halfway back to Memphis by now so I didn't have to worry about my secret getting back to Justin so I made the promise of no more lies and I was grateful not to have to worry about my well-hidden secret coming out of the closet.

38
SANTANA

A few days after our conversation at the hospital, Mike and I decided to take the kids to Incredible Pizza and to my surprise I actually had a terrific time playing around with them and talking to Mike. It wasn't forced so the pressure was off of me to try to make us seem like a picture perfect family.

On the drive home, Mya wanted to know why they were staying at their grandparent's house instead of at home and I told them that I just need some alone time.

"Does that mean that you don't want us any more mommy?" she cried.

"No I will always want you Mya, it just means that mommy has a lot of pressure on her and I just needed a break." I said.

"Just like you take a time out from playing, grown-ups need a time out from time-to-time as well." Mike said softly.

Malik was too busy texting while listening to his iPod to even hear what we were talking about.

"I had a great time tonight." I smiled.

"Yeah, me too. Do you mind if I drop the kids off first so that they can get showered and settled in for the night?" Mike asked.

"Go right ahead." I said, "I want to say hi to mom and dad anyway."

"Mom hasn't been feeling too well lately."

"Oh, has she been to the doctor?"
"Yes, but I don't think that it was good news."
"Is the cancer back?"
Mike shook his head yes as he looked in the rearview mirror at our sleeping daughter and oblivious son. "This time it is more aggressive."
I put my hand to my mouth, "I'm sorry to hear that."
"Please don't mention it you know how private my parents can be."
Mike turned up the music as we rode to his parents' house. His mother was happy to see us together again, but the smile on her face didn't hide the sick that was ravaging through her body.
"It is good to see you."
"Hi mom." I said hugging her tightly.
"Well, well, well…" Mike's father said as he came into the foyer of the large house. "It is good seeing the two of you together as a family, as God intended it."
"Hey dad." I hugged him while ignoring the last comment.
"Dad, I am going to put Mya in bed." Mike said to his father as he carried Mya upstairs, "Malik come on and get in the shower."
I embraced my teenaged son and said, "I miss you baby."
"I miss you too mom." He said without looking up from his important text message.
"Boys and their toys." Mike's mother said as we walked into the formal sitting room, "How are things?"
"Things are going okay."
"Now you know that I don't normally get busy in you and Mike's business, but this separation scares me Santana. I love you like a daughter, but Mike is my son and I don't want to see him get hurt."
Shocked by her statement I said, "I don't intend to hurt Mike; we are just working through some problems."
"Work through them together not apart." Mike's father spoke. "Let all bitterness, and wrath, and anger, and clamor, and evil speaking, be put away from you, with all malice. And be ye kind one to another, tenderhearted, forgiving one another, even as God for Christ's sake hath forgiven you."
Mike walked into the room and cleared his throat, "Mya is in bed and Malik is in the shower; are you ready to go?" he asked me.
"I remember when I first met you; I think that you were fifteen years-old and you were just a shy pretty little thing, but I knew it then that my son had found his wife." Mike's father spoke, "You did good son, now keep doing good and you two work this mess between you out."
Mike's eyes went to mine.

"I have ten brothers and two sisters and we were all married and stayed married until death did a few of them part. Mike you and Santana made a promise before God, honor that promise son."

"We are trying dad." Mike said.

"Good night mom and dad it was nice seeing you again." I said nervously as I stood to leave.

"It was nice to see you too; hopefully the next time we see one another it will be on better terms." His mother said as she hugged me. "Good night."

It was hard going home alone, but I needed more time to sort out what it was that I was doing with Tabitha and what it is that I wanted for myself.

"I need to run in and grab a few suits." Mike said when we pulled up to our house.

"Mike you don't have to explain it to me; this is your house too."

When we got into the house I walked into the kitchen while he went to the bedroom that we once shared and got a few suits out of the closet. I'd poured myself a glass of wine and was standing by the island by the time that he came back down stairs.

"Since when did you start drinking wine?" he asked.

"I have always enjoyed a glass of Moscato or Pinot Noir, Mike." I answered.

"Well we never kept it in the house."

I changed the subject, "I had a nice time tonight; we haven't laughed that much in a long time."

"We really miss you Santana." Mike walked over to me with hunger in his brown eyes, "I have really missed you."

"Mike I…"

Before I could get anything out he pulled me to him and kissed me with the appetite of a starved man and the passion of a lustful mind. Startled, I dropped the glass of Moscato sending it crashing onto the ceramic tile floor where it shattered at our feet. Normally Mike would've been livid and like a mad man rushed to clean the broken glass up, but tonight he was someone else. Releasing me for only a moment Mike looked deep into my eyes then down at the buttons on my cashmere cardigan. With a sweep of his hand he grabbed the sweater and ripped it open exposing a laced pink tank top underneath. Kissing my neck and collarbone Mike began working on my trousers as he fumbled with the belt and buttons. I hadn't seen Mike behave this way in such a long time, but I did not stop him nor slow him down.

Once inside of my pants Mike took his fingers and played with my freshly shaved pussy and smiled. Seeing my usually sedate husband behave this way turned me on; I began undressing while he took off his shirt and pants. We looked like two horny teenagers. Kissing my mouth Mike pushed me against the kitchen island lifting me on top of it where I wrapped my long legs around his body. He dipped low and began sucking my clit first softly then with aggression. With my nails entangled in his curly hair I threw my head back as I could no longer hold in the cries of pain and pleasure that spilled out of my mouth. His dick was as hard as concrete as he slammed into my body vehemently. I backed up, but he wrapped his arms around my waist and pulled me back to him forcing me to take each and every inch of his manhood and each and every thrust of his dick.

"Oh God!" I screamed, "I am about to come!"

"Come for me baby!" Mike moaned as he pounded my body.

Closing my eyes I could see every color of the rainbow, hear every sound in the heavens and taste the sweet sweat that poured down my forehead onto my lips. I gripped his back as the muscles in my thighs and arms contracted, but that didn't stop him he only dug deeper. I couldn't understand the sensations that were running from my spine to each of my limbs, but I didn't care. Mike burrowed deep inside of me holding my legs around his body; he looked at me like a mad dog in heat as he geared up to explode inside of my body sending his own body into a convulsion.

"Shit Santana!" he screamed. "I love you!"

We laid on the cold, hard floor intertwined in each other's arms, surrounded by articles of clothing with shallow breaths, pounding hearts and sweaty brows. Looking at me with softness in his eyes my husband smiled and began playing connect the dots with the light freckles that made a path across the face like he has done so many times before. We didn't speak because there was nothing that needed to be said.

The following day at the office I received a phone call from the company's bank regarding my Visa card. The representative said that they were concerned by unusual purchases on my account and they needed to see if they were valid.

"Five-hundred, thirty-two dollars and fifteen cents was spent at Saks Fifth Avenue in Frontenac, three-hundred, ninety six dollars and nine cents at BCBG also in Frontenac." He said.

My mouth hit the floor when he told me the charges for hotels and restaurants that have been made over the past few days. I couldn't believe that I was so naive as to trust Tabitha with my credit card. Then I remembered the mysterious phone call that I'd gotten a few months

Skeletons

before and how I should have taken that as a que to get out. After telling the representative that I lost my credit card and to deactivate it I went to Tabitha's desk, but she was gone. Furious I walked back into my own office and dialed her cell phone, but I got her voicemail. I should have known better. Mike wanted us to have lunch together so as I was heading out to meet him for lunch I put a sticky note on her computer screen:

We need to talk.

"What's wrong, you seem agitated." Mike asked.

"I lost the company credit card." I answered.

"Oh, well have them deactivate it until you find it. I'm sure that it is at home. Maybe it is on the kitchen floor." He winked.

I smiled.

"I miss you so much Santana." He said holding my hand.

I smiled once more.

"These past few days have been so hard on me and on the kids. I want us to work this out and I want our family back, but I just can't take the secrets any longer."

"Mike I understand all of that, but you have to understand that I can't take feeling unwanted and unloved either."

"I do love you Santana."

"You don't show it."

Sighing Mike admitted, "I guess that I settled into the comfort zone and was kind of ignoring you lately, but baby I promise you that will change. Just be honest and tell me that you are not seeing another man behind my back."

I looked him in his pleading eyes and said, "I swear that there is no other man." In my mind it was not a lie because Tabitha was not a man.

"What about the Visa bill?"

"I am sorry; I've been shopping and going out to eat a lot lately. I guess that I have been running from our problems."

"Baby there shouldn't be anything that we can't discuss with one another."

"I know, but I am tired of arguing."

"I am sorry for my part in this whole thing, but you are my life and I want to make this work. I am in this for life."

Out of the corner of my eye I saw Tabitha come into the restaurant holding hands and laughing with another woman. When she saw me looking at her, she whispered something to the woman then made her way over to our table, but not before letting go of her hand.

"Hello." She smiled, "Hi Mike it's nice seeing you again."

Trying to hide my fury I forced a fake smile and said, "Fancy seeing you here." As my eyes darted from her to her older friend then back to Tabitha again.

"My friend asked me out to lunch and you know that I am not one to turn down a free meal."

Mike looked at Tabitha with contempt.

"Yeah I know how you are." I said dryly.

Tabitha's eyes went from Mike then back to me in an uncomfortable silence, "Well I guess that I will see you back at the office."

"Is she with that woman?" Mike asked in disgust as he looked at Tabitha and her friend snuggle at their booth.

"I guess."

"I can't stand to watch it." He said beckoning the waiter for the check.

"Watch what Mike?"

"I can't understand why a woman would turn to another woman or a man to turn to another man. It's ungodly and disgusting."

I knew that Mike didn't care of the homosexual lifestyle, but I never knew how much it disgusted him. The look of disdain was written all over his face.

"If one of my children were to tell me that they preferred the same sex, I'd never speak to them again."

I swallowed my tilapia with a hard gulp, "I never knew that you felt this strongly against homosexuality Mike."

"I hate it." He spit. "Wrongdoers will not inherit the kingdom of God. Do not be deceived, neither the sexually immoral nor idolaters nor adulterers nor men who have sex with other men no thieves nor the greedy nor drunkards nor slanderers nor swindlers will inherit the kingdom of God." He quoted from the Bible.

"The Bible also says that we are not to judge Mike."

"Stop defending them Santana." He pulled money out of his wallet and threw it on the table, "I can't take this any longer, let's go."

The cold weather whipped through my thin shirt as I rushed behind Mike trying to keep up with his fast stride, "Mike slow down."

"What exactly was the nature of your friendship with that woman, Santana?" he asked.

"She is my assistant."

"But you have been hanging out with her lately."

"She is just a friend Mike."

"Yeah whatever." He rolled his eyes as we got inside of his car; Mike drove me back to work in silence, I couldn't tell what was going on in his head, but I know that it couldn't have been good thoughts.

Skeletons

Tabitha walked into my office as soon as she saw the post it note on her computer, "You wanted to see me?"

Looking at the smug look on her face I directed her to close the door. "Mike looked pissed off."

"He isn't the only one. Where is my credit card Tabitha?" I asked.

"What credit card?"

"The one that you took from me at Maggiano's the other night."

"Oh, the one that you gave to me."

"I didn't give you shit."

"Yes you did."

"Okay whatever, where is it because I see that you took it upon yourself to go on a shopping spree."

"What is this about Tabitha? Are you jealous that I was out with Christy this afternoon?" she asked as if she didn't know.

"No, I'm mad that you were out on some sort of shopping spree with my card!"

"You handed it to me."

"I was upset about my friend getting shot and you took it to pay for our meal."

"Why didn't you ask for it back?" she was playing a game that she has played many times before.

"You are lucky that I don't turn you in."

"Why would you turn me in Santana, are you a lover scorned? Jealous that I dumped you and moved on with someone new?" the smug look returned.

"Excuse me!" I rose from my desk.

"This isn't the first time I've been through this and I'm sure that it won't be the last. You older women kill me with how territorial you can be. First you wine and dine me then as soon as shit turns sour you want all of your shit back!"

"Tabitha, you really don't know me. You have one minute to give me back my fucking card, two minutes to pack all of your shit and three minutes to get the hell out of here."

Tabitha laughed, "The thing is you don't know me." Held up her iPhone and played a video of her lying on the bed with our male partner caressing her naked breast and my face buried deep in her pussy. "Smile for the camera?" she said on the video as she laughed. I looked up at the camera, lips wet from her juices, eyes glazed from the drugs that we'd taken and I smiled.

Tabitha smirked at the look on my face and said softly, "Who has more to lose?" Turning, she sashayed out of my office.

Shimeka R. McFadden

39
ASTERIA

Pandia had been acting very strange towards me, but she came by to take Latif to the park with her and little Keith while Eric and I chilled around the house. It was nice to finally have a boyfriend as someone to call my own, but I was always on edge that he would find out about Keith and I.
My sister returned with Latif an hour after Eric left.
"Hey sis, come in." I offered as she stood on the porch.
"No, I'm good." She said flatly.
"Is everything okay?"
"Yep. I'll see you at work tomorrow." She turned and walked away.
Latif and I visited Jovanna while Justin was at work. Jovanna was discharged from the hospital three days ago and I wanted to give her some time to rest before I went to see her. I knocked on the door, a visiting nurse answered and let me in. Jovanna was lying across the couch while the nurse took her vitals and checked her wound.
"Hey love, how are you?" I asked as I took Latif's coat and hat off.
"Tired and in pain." She said drowsily, "Hi Latif." She smiled at my son.
I watched as the nurse finished her work, had Jovanna sign a few pieces of paper then left.
"How are things with Eric?" she asked.

With a huge smile on my face, "Great, he is such a wonderful man Jovanna. I didn't think that any of those existed anymore."

"How are things with your sister and Keith? The last time I saw her she was pissed off about him running out on her."

"That will be the story of their lives." I laughed, "I guess things are alright, she has been acting kind of strange towards me though."

"Why do you think that is?"

"I don't know, maybe because I have been spending so much time with Eric and not enough wiping her tears."

"That is what sisters are for." She grunted as she tried to sit herself up, I came over and helped her get situated.

"Have you talked to Santana?"

"She came over the other day and made dinner and told me about your arguement."

I sighed, "I didn't mean for it to have gone that far."

"I know, but you two have been friends forever Asteria and it is time that you made up. Trust me life is too precious to waste time."

"I know, but Santana has been so wrapped up in Tabitha that she pushes her real friends off to the side."

"What is up with Tabitha?"

"Tabitha is a gold-digging whore who preys on married women. I did a little asking around and found out that she has ruined a few marriages between associates that I know."

Jovanna laughed, "Do you think that she is munching Santana's carpet?"

I laughed, "Yeah right Santana doesn't even swing that way, but for the life of me I can't understand why she would hang with someone like Tabitha. That bitch has been around the block more times than the Good Humor Man."

"Wow."

"We do need to talk because I miss her." I said looking at my son play, he did look a lot like his father and I wondered if that was why my sister has been acting standoffish towards me lately.

"I am so glad that you stopped by though. I need someone to do my laundry because Justin cannot wash worth a damn."

I laughed, "No problem, just point me in the right direction."

I finished washing Jovanna's clothes, cleaned her kitchen and made pork chops and green beens. After we ate I took Latif home to put him to bed.

A few nights later while lying in bed, I received a text message from Keith:

Skeletons

Hi
I text back:
What now Keith?
Keith:
What are you doing?
Me:
What does it matter?
Keith:
I want to see you.
Me:
I told you that it was over.
Keith:
Please let me see you just one last time.
Me:
Only if you promise to leave me alone.
Keith:
I promise. Meet me at the Red Roof Inn off of 270

I called the babysitter to come over and watch Latif while I went to the hotel. Keith was nothing special to me any longer so I didn't feel the need to dress up for him as I once did; throwing on an old sweat suit I drove to the hotel to meet Keith. As much as I hate to admit it I did missed Keith, but I didn't miss him enough to put up with his bullshit for the rest of my life. I pulled up next to his truck that was parked in the back of the hotel and walked in.
As I went to the front desk to ask for his room the clerk looked at me and said, "I'm sorry, but we don't have anyone by that name." irritated I turned around and there stood Pandia with tears pouring down her face; we stood face-to-face my secret fully exposed.
"It's been you all along." She cried, "How could you?"
I was speechless. There was so much that I wanted to say, but the words wouldn't come out.
"You are not only my sister, but we shared a womb together and here you are fucking my man. I trusted you, I cried on your shoulder and you knew all along." She spat.
"Pandia I…"
"Don't you dare say a word!" she yelled with her finger pointed in my face.
"I am sorry." I cried. "This wasn't supposed to happen."
"How dare you stand there and cry. How dare you! After all of these years you knew! You were getting child support from my husband

behind my back."

The clerk came up to us, "Excuse me, but I am going to have to ask you to leave."

"Don't worry I'm going." Pandia tightened her coat and stormed out of the double doors.

I couldn't move, I only stood there and cried.

40
JOVANNA

I'd been held up in the house since I'd been discharged; Justin decided to take me out to dinner at the Drunken Fish for sushi. I was still in pain, but with the right amount of painkillers I felt good enough to get out of the house.

"How are you feeling?" he asked when we sat at our table.
"I'm alright." I grunted. "I've been better."
"I am glad to hear that Jovanna came over and did the laundry because I didn't want to hear your mouth about me bleaching your DKNY again."
"I could've killed you."
Justin laughed.
"Justin thanks for being so understanding and I am sorry for hiding this from you. This has been very difficult for me, I don't know if I would have gotten through this without you."
"You are welcome Jovanna." he smiled brightly, "Now let's not talk about that right now. Let's have a good night instead."
"Now, can I get some sake?" I smiled ready to have a drink and some fun. It felt good not to have to look behind my back all of the time.
"You wait here while I get the car." Justin offered after dinner. I fought off the pain that was beginning to return as I struggled to put on my coat and scarf as I waited for Justin to pull up in the warm car.

After waiting ten minutes I decided to see what was taking him so long, I walked out to the parking lot where we parked the car and that is when I saw Chad's red Cadillac sitting next to our car. Panicked my eyes darted to the left of Chad's car where Justin was fighting for his life.

As fast as my body could manage, I limped across the parking lot, Chad held onto a long blade as Justin tried to fight him off.

"Justin!" I called which was a mistake because when he looked over at me Chad took the blade, plunging it into Justin's body sending him falling to the ground. I screamed ignoring the strong pain in my arms, back and leg as I ran as fast as my body could take me to where he lay on the ground.

Upon seeing me coming for him Chad smiled, "See Marquita I told you that I'd get what you took from me back."

"I gave you your money!" I yelled.

"It was never about the money! I have money! You took my reputation away from me; it took me a lifetime to build that up and now it is gone. Because of you I lost my respect, because of you I am a weak fool playing the role of a pimp. You took away my life and now I return the favor." Chad's eyes were as cold as the air that circled around our bodies as he lunged towards me with the long, blood-covered knife pointed at my heart. Dodging him, he slipped on a piece of ice losing his balance, dropping the knife. Living in Memphis Chad was unaware of winter fashion in the ice and snow. His purple gators were not match for the slippery substance that surrounded us.

With adrenaline keeping me from feeling the pain that was shooting through my healing body I acted quickly and dove for the weapon, suddenly slipping myself barely missing landing on top of Chad as he struggled to gain his footing in order to get up. I called out in pain as my wounded body came crashing down upon the ground.

Two sets of eyes, riddled with fear and pain looked at the knife as two sets of hands clawed at the ice and two sets of legs kicked at one another as we fought to regain control on the ground as we competed for the shiny steel blade. Chad grabbed at my sprawling legs as I attempted to crawl toward the knife which was almost within arm's reach. I could hear him struggle to grab me, but the pain in his shattered knee and age kept him from being successful.

I grabbed the blade in my right hand while I regained my footing. Walking towards him as he laid out of breath on the frigid pavement; a cheap pimp in a five-hundred dollar suit. With all of the strenght that I had left I brought my boot down upon his body as it landed hard on his chest. Chad let out a loud groan as he rolled over to his side unable to catch his breath. Years of expensive Cuban cigars, dark cognac and rough sex finally caught up with him. The man who I once feared and thought to be invincible now lay at my feet unable to even stand and continue to fight me.

Holding the blade in my hand I waved it at him, "I didn't take anything from you because it was never yours to begin with. You took my life from me when I was too young and naïve to know what life was and when I asked for my life back you refused so I took it."

"Fuck you bitch!" Chad spat a thin trail of blood clung to his bottom lip refusing to hit the ground.

I could hear Justin moan out in pain as he lay on the icy street still bleeding from his wound.

"You think that you are better than me now; you were nothing when you were working the pole at the Honey Lounge until I made you something! I made you who you are now without me you would still be turning tricks for dollars in Memphis or just like your lousy crack head parents!"

Justin moaned again.

Chad strguuled as he made it onto his feet, "I should have killed you when I had the chance, but that was my fault, but trust me I won't make that mistake again Marquita." Chad lunged toward me with his arms outstretched. He had ahold of me around my neck, but this time instead of falling I plunged the long, steel blade deep into his chest as he attempted to choke my life away from me. Chad dropped his arms and held the spot where the knife made a home of flesh and bone. The look of agony, fear and regret were in his stony eyes as he fell to the ground and a pool of fresh blood poured out of his body and onto the ground where he lay.

"Drop the knife!" I heard a cop yell. I couldn't take my eyes off of Chad, this time I had to see him die I couldn't leave this up to chance like I did ten years ago. The knife hit the concrete, but my eyes never left the sight of my ex-pimp, the man I once loved as he wrestled with the angel of death until he finally lost.

"Turn around and put your hands on your head!"

I blinked my eyes as I entered back to reality to find myself surrounded by police and blinking lights. I looked for Justin, but the paramedics were tending to his injuries. Doing as the officer told I put my hands on top of my head and allowed them to arrest me; my only regret was that Justin was fighting for his life because finally I was free.

41
SANTANA

Asteria and I walked into the hospital together as our men followed. Our strides were strong yet filled with worry as this was the second time our friend was attacked this month and we wondered what was going on.
I cried into Mikes arms as Asteria asked about Jovanna and Keith as mad as I was at her I wouldn't allow our argument keep us from being there for one another. We waited around for an hour until Jovanna walked out the grimace on her face told us that she was in a lot of pain. She embraced me then pulled Asteria in as we stood holding one another in slience just as friends are supposed to do.
"How is Justin?" I asked.
"The doctors said that the knife missed any vital organs and that he should be fine."
"What is going on Jovanna, this is the third time that you were attacked?" I asked.
Jovanna cried, "I can't talk to you about it right now, please give me some time."
"There shouldn't be secrets between friends." I reminded her.
"I know Santana, but if you would allow me some time…"
"Take your time; go tend to your man." Asteria looked at me sternly, her

eyes begging me to let up on her friend.
"I feel like my life is in shambles."
Mike came up and hugged Jovanna, "Let's pray for healing and clarity." Holding hands and interlocking our fingers we all bowed our heads as Mike lead us in prayer and at that moment, with the amount of compassion that my husband extended towards my best friend, I knew that I'd made a huge mistake and I wanted him back in my life forever.
We left the hospital and drove back to our home where Mike and I first tore each other's clothes off as we fucked on the living room couch, then we showered together with him taking me from behind in the shower, finally ending in our marital bed where we made passionate love falling asleep holding each other.
The following day at work I didn't say anything to Tabitha, but she held a smile on her face the entire day. I wonder if she tried using my credit card again because I put a fraud alert on it so if she did the purchase would decline and the authorities would be notified. That afternoon I was called into Mr. Gold's office for an urgent meeting. I didn't know what was going on, but as I walked out of my office I saw Tabitha passing me with tears in her eyes.
When I got into the large corner office, there sat Mr. Gold, Niles Bergenstein, Mr. Gold's Vice President and Julie.
"Santana, please close the door behind you and have a seat." Mr. Gold said sternly.
I did as I was told taking seat in the large leather chair identical to the one that Julie was seated in to my right.
"A very serious matter has been brought to my attention." He continued, "You know that fraternizing between members of my management team and their employees is strictly prohibited."
"Yes, Mr. Gold I understand that clearly."
"With that being said, what is your relationship with Tabitha?"
"She is my assistant."
"No, what is your personal relationship with her?" Mr. Bergenstein asked.
"We don't have a personal relationship Mr. Bergenstein as I stated before she is my assistant."
"According to Ms. Grey, you two have a very close personal relationship so close that you granted her access your corporate credit card where she made several expensive purchases." He said holding up a copy of the credit card bill.
I shifted in my seat.
"What is the nature of the relationship between you and Ms. Gray?" Mr. Gold asked again.

"She is a friend." I whispered.

"According to Ms. Grey the two of you are involved in a sexual relationship. Is that correct?"

I was too embarrassed to answer.

"According to Ms. Grey, you paid for her companionship through dinners, shopping, hotels and monetary gifts. She informed us that you paid her car note three months in advance."

"Tabitha was a friend in need and I helped her out."

"Were you involved with her sexually?" Julie asked.

"I don't feel the need to answer that question which is my personal business that has nothing to do with this company." I looked at Julie as if she'd lost her mind; despite her Executive Secretary title she was merely an assistant and I still out-ranked her.

Mr. Gold removed his Foster Grant bifocals, "It becomes the business of my company when it affects your work and it has affected our finances due to the fact that she has had access to your credit card to make personal purchases at your behest."

"I inadvertently handed it to her and I've asked for it back, but she refuses."

"Why didn't you come to me about this, if this is truly what happened?"

"I was ashamed." I answered.

Mr. Gold sighed deeply, "You are a good employee, but I cannot go against company policy so I have no choice, but to displace you from employment within our company."

My mouth fell open, "Mr. Gold, I've been with you for over ten years!"

"I know and that is what hurts the most, but if I look the other way for you then I'd have to do it for others and I simply cannot do that. I am sorry Santana." Mr. Gold stood, Mr. Bergenstein and Julie followed.

"Please have your office cleaned out by the end of the day." Mr. Bergenstein put. "It was nice working with you."

Fighting back tears I walked back to my office only to find Tabitha sitting at her desk with that same smug expression written on her face. I walked over to her reached my hand back and landed it across her face. Tabitha fell backwards with her head landing in the black, standard issue office trash can.

"You knew what you were doing all along!" I yelled. "I should've followed my gut and never befriended a scandalous bitch such as you!"

"I didn't force you to do anything." Tabitha said as she stood up and straightens her outfit. "You entered into this by your own free will. You were lonely, you were under sexed and desperate. I gave you what you wanted and I don't recall forcing you to do anything!"

We held the attention of the entire office and security was on their way.
"Tabitha, I feel sorry for you. You seek people out in their time of need and you use them until they catch on to your deceitful little games then you try to ruin them."
"I don't know what you are talking about Santana! I was your friend, I can't help that you have homosexual tendencies that you don't even understand for yourself. I cannot help that you needed to use drugs in order to cope with going home to your husband and children at the end of the day."
"Fuck you!" I lunged at her once again, but the husky security officer grabbed my arm and pushed me back.
"It's time to go." He said.
"I need to get my purse out of my office first." I huffed. I couldn't believe that I allowed myself to lose my cool like that.
I grabbed my purse, coat, pictures of the Mike and the kids and my degree off of the wall and walked out of the office with my head held high. Tabitha sat in her chair with alligator tears running down her face as she played the victim as the entire office was held captive by her performance.
Take a bow.
What was I going to tell Mike? I thought as I drove home in a mad fury. Mike and I discussed him and the children moving back home while we worked on our issues through Christian marital counseling with a Pastor that his father recommended. As I parked my van my cellphone alerted me to a new multimedia message. I opened it, my eyes widened and I suddenly felt sick.
"How do I taste baby?" Tabitha's voice came across and the jittery camera panned to me licking my lips with her juices fresh around my mouth.
"You taste like butterscotch." I moaned.
"Do I taste better than your husband?"
"Who?"
"Mike, do I taste better than Mike?" she asked in a drunken laughter.
"Mike who?" I smiled as I buried my face back between her thighs.
Tears escaped my eyes as I watched how starved I looked.
I looked up as Mike was watching the same video on his own phone as he too cried tears of a marriage pushed to the edge and could not be saved.
Mike removed most of his things from our house. That night as I sat alone in my bedroom crying because of the deceit that I locked in my closet I lost not only my job, but also my dignity, respect and most importantly I lost my family.

42
ASTERIA

My insides hurt as I drove home from the hotel that night and now sitting here in the hospital waiting on the news about Justin, I felt as if I needed to be admitted into one of the hospital beds in the psych ward. I couldn't believe that Pandia knew about Keith and I. The only thing that I could do was cry.

"Hey baby are you alright?" Eric asked as we drove home from the hospital in silence.

"My stomach hurts just a little."

"When we get to your house I will make you some tea to settle your bowels." He offered.

"No, Eric I think that it would be best if you just dropped me off at home and you went to your own house."

"Wow." He breathed, "I didn't see that one coming."

"I'm sorry it's just that I am so tired and I have a lot on my plate so I want to be alone tonight." I softened my tone and rubbed his back.

"If you say so." He said picking up speed in the car.

Once inside of my house I asked the babysitter to stay while I took a hot shower. I felt numb and alone with no one knowing my secret; I had no one to talk to. I thought that I was done crying myself to sleep when I ended things with Keith.

I felt like a moving target the following morning when I walked into the salon. All eyes were on me. Pandia was sitting in her chair smoking a cigarette and drinking out of a bottle of Citron Patron.

"Well, well, well look at what the cat drug in." she slurred, "My twin sister Asteria. You guys know one thing about twins is that we can tell when the other one is in pain? Yeah, that is the truth; I remember when we were twelve and Asteria was in The Girl Scouts when she broke her arm I felt that shit before I even knew that she was hurt."

"She has been like this all morning." Aaron whispered to me, "What is going on Asteria?"

Pandia stepped up to me and pointed in my chest, "See sister, my pain is your pain and your pain is mine."

Londyn tried to take the bottle from Pandia, but she pulled away. "Don't touch me Londyn! I love you like a sister, but you could never truly be my sister."

"Come on Pandia, let's go inside of my office and talk about this." I offered, but she went on.

"Do you know why you could never be my sister Londyn?" she slurred.

"Why?" Londyn asked clearly irritated.

"Because you are too good of a person and you have morals, respect oh and you would never fuck my husband." She took a swig from the bottle in her hand.

My head dropped low as everyone in the salon looked at me in shock.

"What is she talking about Asteria?" Londyn asked.

"Pandia, please let's talk about this in private. Please don't do this here."

"We shared a womb for nine months and apparently we also were sharing a man for the past three years."

Londyn looked at me with disgust, "Is this true Asteria? Were you sleeping with Keith?"

Tears rolled from my eyes and hit the black ceramic tiled floor, "Yes."

Aaron's hands clasped over his mouth, "Oh my God."

"Asteria how could you?" Londyn asked as she moved away from me. "That is your sister."

Pandia took a long swig of the bitter tasting liquor and garbled, "But that is not all! Do you want to tell them the good part or should I?"

I was silent.

"My son has a brother and his name is Latif. Our sons are not only cousins, but also brothers. Now ain't that some shit!"

"What!" Aaron exclaimed, "Now this is too much!"

"The thing is I can't even blame you Asteria, because you have some serious mommy issues. You always felt as if mom didn't love you as much as she loved me no matter how much you over achieved and tried to outshine me." Pandia poked me in my forehead forcing my head back, exposing the flood of tears that were streaming down my face. "Truthfully mommy loved you very much. She was proud of you for all that you accomplished, but she knew that you were the strong one out of us. She knew that you would make it, but she was unsure about me; that is why she rushed me into marrying Keith because she felt that I needed a man to take care of me." She laughed the laugh of madness and pain.

There I stood, exposed with nothing to say.

"Keith doesn't want you. He will never leave me. I curse the day that you were born." Pandia said with her nose against my nose, the scent of cigarettes and alcohol escaping her breath, attacking my nostrils.

Pandia grabbed her coat and stormed out of the salon.

"She can't drive home like that!" Aaron said as he grabbed his own coat and ran after Pandia.

I looked at Londyn who held up her hand and said, "I don't even have words for you. I have a client in fifteen minutes."

Feeling like a fool I walked to my office where I stayed for the duration of the day.

Eric came over later that evening even though I'd been ignoring his calls and texts. He wanted to know what was going on and why I was acting shady towards him. I curled up on the couch with a blanket thrown over me while Latif was in his room playing. I couldn't hold it in any longer, I had to tell someone the truth.

"I am not who you think I am Eric." I said with tears in my eyes, "I am a horrible person."

Puzzled, Eric asked "What do you mean?"

"I never meant for any of this to happen, but I never tried to stop it either."

"Asteria, what is going on?"

"I have been sleeping with my sister's husband for the past three years and Latif is his son." I admitted, as bad as I felt it was also a relief to finally say it out loud to someone.

Eric looked at me in disbelief then put his face in his greasy hands.

"You can hate me now; everyone else does."

He remained silent for a few moments then looked me deep in my eyes and said, "I don't hate you. Does your sister know about this?"

"Yes, she recently found out. I never meant to hurt her."

"This is deep Asteria. Are you still seeing him?"

"No I ended it shortly before meeting you; I just couldn't do it any longer."

"What is your sister saying?"

"Well, she cursed me out at the salon this morning so basically she hates me."

"I doubt that she hates you, she is just angry as she should be. You deceived her, she is hurt."

I rose from the couch and yelled, "What do you want me to do!"

"Show some compassion Asteria!"

"She has always had it all; she had the grades, she had the looks and she mom's love!" I cried, "All I wanted was to have the love that she had, but he didn't love me, he just used me."

"You allowed yourself to be used!" he yelled back, startling me, "So now what?" Eric stood in my face.

"I don't know Eric. She is hurting so bad, but I'm hurting too."

"Tell her." He suggested.

"I can't, she won't answer her phone."

"Then go where she is and tell her until she listens." Eric wrapped his arms around me, "That is your sister, your twin and you two share a bond that is unlike any other. You need one another; don't let this ruin your bond."

"You can leave if you want, I will understand." I cried.

Eric looked confused, "Why would I leave you?"

"Because I am a terrible person; what type of person fucks her own sister's husband?"

"The kind of person who needs a love of her own." He kissed me passionately. "I guarantee you that you will never sleep with him again." As bad as I felt, Eric had a way of making me feel really good about myself; I knew that I would have to speak to Pandia sooner or later and I wanted the support of my girls, Santana and Jovanna to back me up.

43
JOVANNA

The doorbell rang frantically as I rushed as fast as I could to answer it; my body was still in a lot of pain, but with the right amount of painkillers and alcohol I could ignore it.
"Where is my son?" Justin's mother demanded as soon as I opened the front door. The smell of White Diamonds walked in before she did.
"Hello Mrs. Dobbins; Justin is in bed resting."
She walked into our house with her nose in the air as she looked around our disorganized place; since I'd been shot and Justin stabbed we really didn't have the strength to clean up. She removed the black leather coat and matching driving gloves, carefully sitting them on the back of the couch with disapproval written all over her face.
"What kind of bullshit did you get my son involved in?" The salt-n-pepper haired woman asked as she continued to eyeball the house.
"Excuse me?" I was offended.
"My son is a good kid, he was raised in a rough neighborhood, with guns and drugs, yet he didn't get into any trouble until he met you. What did you get him involved in Jovanna?"
"Mom lay off." Justin said as he slowly walked out of our bedroom holding his wound. His curly, brown hair was disheveled and his skin was more pale than usual from losing so much blood.

Mrs. Dobbins hugged her son tightly, "How are you?"

"I am fine." He said holding his side. "I don't like the way that you talk to Jovanna mom."

"You are my son and I don't like the fact that she got you involved into something that got you hurt."

"Jovanna had nothing to do with me getting stabbed; it was just some random guy." He said dismissing his mother's claim.

Looking at me through skeptical eyes she said, "I find it strange how first your house gets broken into, then she gets shot in a random act of violence then not even a month later you end up stabbed! There is something fishy with the picture and I know that it isn't my son."

"Look, you can't come in my home disrespecting me like that." I fussed back.

Laughing arrogantly she said, "Your home, look honey this was my home when we first moved to St. Louis, when we got our current home built Justin's father gave this one to him as a graduation gift. This home of yours is still in my name."

I looked at my pain-riddled fiancé and asked, "Is that true?"

"Yes, I haven't had the chance to change the deed yet." Justin managed.

"This is technically my home and I can have your black ass tossed onto the street; right back where you came from."

I felt foolish; I couldn't believe that Justin hadn't told me that our house was still in his parent's name.

"I don't see why he is marrying you; you are clearly cut from a different type of cloth than he is." She continued, "Justin when will you learn that these type of girls only bring you trouble and bad luck?"

"Is this how you feel?" I asked Justin. "Do I only bring you trouble and bad luck?"

The grimace on his face told me that he was in too much pain to answer my question.

"You need to find you a decent woman to bring into our family and make some pure and pretty babies." She continued. "I don't know why you always got mixed up in this crowd. This is why we moved you away from the coast."

I looked at my fiancé in disbelief as he lay there with agnoy written all over his face and body. I went into my bedroom, changed clothes, put on my tennis shoes and pulled a hat over my messy hair then walked out of the house into the cold air leaving Justin with his mom. Not knowing where to go I called Asteria and Santana to meet me for breakfast. Santana didn't answer, but Asteria said that she was on her way.

I thought that with the death of Chad my nightmare was over, but now

Skeletons

there would be questions. As much as I love Justin, I was not prepared to lie to him any longer and I knew that was a great risk to take.

"I have to tell you something." I said as soon as my somber looking friend sat down at the table.

"I have to tell you something too." She said.

Santana walked into the café wearing a red jogging suit, her long weave pulled back into a ponytail underneath a St. Louis Cardinals hat. Her eyes were swollen and bloodshot, "I have something to say."

I was glad that things between she and Asteria have died down because that was one less thing that I had to deal with.

"Who goes first?" I asked.

"You called us here, so you go ahead." Asteria said.

"We always said that we were like sisters and that we were so close that we didn't keep secrets form one another. Well, I have been hiding a skeleton in my closet, but now it is time for it to come out." I began, "I have been to hell and back trying to keep this hidden, but look at where it has gotten me, I was shot and my fiancé was stabbed." I cried, "I just can't hide this any longer."

"My name isn't Jovanna and I am not from New York. My name is Marquita and I am from Memphis. I've been running from my past because I didn't want you guys to think any less of me."

"Why would we think less of you? We love you Jovanna." Santana said as she held my hand.

"Or should we call you Marquita." Asteria joked.

"The guy who shot me and stabbed Justin, his name was Chad and he was my pimp. My parents were addicted more to crack than they were to me so I ran away at the age of sixteen. I began working at a strip club until I met Chad. He treated me better than my parents ever did and I fell in love with him. Soon I began turning tricks for him."

"Ten years ago I stole over ten-thousand dollars from him and he was back to collect his money and to take my life." The tears were flowing so fast that I couldn't blink them away they hit the table forming a small puddle. "I didn't lose my engagement ring; I pawned it and maxed out my credit cards in order to pay him back. But for Chad it was never about the money, he wanted revenge because I ruined his life and now he ruined mine. I thought that I could run and hide from my past, but you can't run from who you truly are. I was, am and will always be a prostitute named Marquita."

"Wow." Asteria breathed, "And I thought that I was having a bad week."

Santana rolled her eyes, "Honey I know who you are, you are a sweet, caring, loving and giving person who never harmed anyone. You are my friend and I only know you as Jovanna so that is who you will always be in my eyes."

"I love you Jovanna; I don't know that Marquita girl." Asteria said.

"I know that I may seem to be making light of this, but I am glad that you told us because we didn't know what was going on with you. Hell, I thought you have some mob ties or something. I accept you for who you are, you are like my sister and I will never judge you based off of what you did in the past."

"Does Justin know?" Santana asked.

"No, I don't know how to tell him."

"Just like you told us, just do it."

"What if he leaves?" I cried, "I love him so much that I couldn't take it if he left me."

"And if he leaves you will know that he was not in it for better or for worse honey." She answered.

"If he leaves then we will be right here with you, wiping another puddle of tears off of the table. That is what friends are for." Asteria said as she wiped away the puddle of tears.

"Thank you for understanding and being here for me." I smiled as I wiped my eyes.

"No problem, we love you girl." Asteria said as they reached over and hugged me.

The waitress came over and took our orders, strangely none of us felt like eating much. Sitting in silence for a moment, Santana let out a deep sigh.

"I guess I will go next." She said, "I have been keeping a secret as well. Mike and I have been together since we were in high school but lately things between us have been very strained. I've been feeling trapped and I was looking for a way out. Mike and the kids were suffocating me and I know that you guys have been wondering about my relationship with Tabitha, being with her breathed new life inside of me. I was having an affair with Tabitha and that affair cost me not only my relationship with my husband, but it also cost me my job."

My jaw hit my plate, "You have been sleeping with your assistant Santana?"

"I never intended for it to go this far, but I guess that the excitement of it got me in over my head."

"I told you that there was something that I didn't like about that heifer!" Asteria shot. "Does Mike know?"

Tears formed in Santana's already swollen eyes, "He found out as he was moving back in. Mike said that he wants a divorce as soon as possible."

Skeletons

I held my friend as she balled into her pancake breakfast. "I am sorry to hear that."

"He isn't willing to try to work it out for the sake of the children?" Asteria asked.

She cried harder, "No, he hates homosexuality and once he makes up his mind about something that is generally the end of it." She blew her nose on a napkin, "I can't believe that I got myself into this mess at my age."

Asteria said, "You may not have Mike, but you will always have us Santana. If you need anything or just a shoulder to cry on, we are here. I know that you and I don't always see eye-to-eye on things, but I love you like a sister and I will never turn my back on you."

"Thank you Asteria that means a lot."

Asteria broke down and cried, "It is funny how I talk about friendship and sisterhood, when in fact I am not much of a friend or a good sister."

"What do you mean?" I asked.

"For the last three years I have been having an affair with a married man, an affair resulted in Latif." Asteria took a gulp of her orange juice, "I have been sleeping with Keith."

I dropped my fork in the sticky syrup, "Pandia's husband Keith?"

Santana shook her head, "No, please tell me that you haven't been sleeping with your sister's husband Asteria."

"I never meant for it to happen, it just came about and I couldn't stop it. Keith had a hold on me and I was in love with him. He kept promising me that he was going to leave my sister and that we were going to move to Seattle to begin a new life; and I was foolish enough to believe the bastard. I ended things with him after I met Eric and I was prepared to keep my secret hidden, but it was too late."

"Pandia found out?"

"Yes; when she confronted me at the salon I couldn't even defend myself. That is my sister and I love her more than anything, but I am such a bad person that I allowed a man to come in between us like that."

"Damn I knew that Keith was a dog, but I didn't know that he was that foul." Santana said, "I am quite sure that Pandia will forgive you eventually."

"Would you forgive me?" I asked my freckle-faced friend, "Would you forgive your twin sister if she not only fucked your man, but also had a child by him? I know that I wouldn't." Asteria questioned, "All of the while I'm sitting there listening to her cry about how he didn't come home until five in the morning or how he smelled of perfume when all of the while he was with me." She reflected, "How forgivable is that?"

"Don't beat yourself up about this; Keith is also to blame." I tried to console my friend.

"Keith is not Pandia's sister, I am!" she emitted, "And now I have to live with this for the rest of my life." She cried.

"Talk to her." Santana suggested, "I am sure that you can work this out."

"There is no talking to her right now." Asteria looked through her purse taking out a wad of money then tossing it on the table in front of us, "I am going to sell my half of the salon and move."

"Running away is not going to solve the problem."

"No, but at least I won't have to look in the face of the person whom I betrayed every day." She put on her coat, "I have to go, but thanks for listening."

Santana and I sat and watched in awe as Asteria made a quick exit from the restaurant and we didn't utter a word.

44
ASTERIA

Pandia didn't answer any of the fifty plus calls and text messages that I sent to her; I even tried calling Keith's phone, but he just hit the ignore button. I waited until the salon was empty and I moved all of my belongings out of the salon. I hated leaving Gods and Goddesses, but after what I did I couldn't imagine staying. I had not told Eric about my plans to move back to Phoenix and as much as I hated to play him like this I didn't deserve a good man like him.
"It looks like it is just going to be you and me little guy." I told Latif as we played with his toys on the floor of his bedroom. "I promise that I will never hurt you."
There was a knock at the door, and to my surprise it was Pandia and little Keith.
"Are you going to invite me in?" she hissed as she held her son on one hip.
Moving out of her way I let her into the warm house.
"We are not going to stay long, I just wanted little Keith to come by and play with his brother." I could tell that it hurt her to acknowledge my son as her son's brother.
"That is fine." I said without looking her in the eyes. "Would you like something to eat or drink?" I asked.

She shook her head no while looking around my house as if she were looking for something, "It is hard for me to even be here, wondering which couch, chair or floor that you fucked my husband on." She said. "How could you?"

"I don't know it just happened."

"NO! You don't get off that easily Asteria!" she yelled. "All of your life you have been taking the easy way out to everything, but not this time. This time you are going to explain to me how it is that you could work with me every day, how you could sit there and listen to me cry my eyes out about my husband and yet know that you were the one fucking him! How could you?"

"I loved him Pandia! I fell in love with Keith. He made so many promises…"

Throwing her hands up she said, "He is always making promises Asteria! That is how he operates. Keith is a man who will tell you anything that you want to hear just to get what he wants from you. Did you really think that he would leave me?"

"He said that he would and that we were moving to Seattle to start over. I believed him."

"So you would be willing to take my son's father away from him? You loved this man so much that you would do this to me?"

"At the time yes, but then I began to feel bad about it and I didn't want to be with him any longer."

"When did that happen; after you finally met someone of your own? Or was it after I stopped crying over him and started paying attention to shit? It is hard for me to believe that after three years you grew a damn conscious?"

"I saw all of the hurt in your eyes and then when he started sleeping with Keisha I knew that Keith would never leave and that he was just playing games. I tried breaking things off with him Pandia, but he kept coming at me."

"You shouldn't have ever slept with my husband to begin with." She muffed me in my face sending my head snapping back. "I hate you so much right now. You or your bastard son will never be welcome in my house again." She spat. "Don't ever call me again; as far as I'm concerned you do not exist."

Tears stung my eyes as I tried to control my emotions, "I am your sister Pandia. I never meant to hurt you or little Keith."

"You hurt me and you saw that hurt almost every day! You and that trifling husband of mine sat up laughing in my face knowing all of the while the secret that the two of you shared. It was one thing finding out that Keith was sleeping with Keisha, but to find out that he was sleeping with my own damn sister was something totally different." She said, "I trusted you more than I trusted him and I loved you more than I loved him. If I ever see you in the salon, I might stab you with a pair of shears." She seethed through clinched teeth, "That is a promise sister."

"I feel as if you are putting all of the blame on me; what about Keith?" I cried. "He is the one that you married; he is the one that made a vow to be loyal to you."

Crossing her trembling arms across her chest my sister confessed, "I allow Keith to sleep around on me. After we got married my husband's sexual appetite was more than I could handle so I told him that he could have sex with other women as long as it didn't interfere with our relationship. At first it didn't hurt as bad because he kept his affairs under control, only fucking other women every once in a while and not allowing them to affect our home. However, after I had little Keith his daddy began getting out of control and disrespectful towards me by not making it home and taking phone calls while we were together."

"Why would you allow him to cheat on you Pandia?"

"I thought that it would help!" she said with tears bucketing down her face, "I thought that if I allowed him to be a man and sow his oats every once in a while that it would bring us closer and that he would love me, but I was wrong. I thought that I would be able to handle the fact that my husband slept with other women, but I was wrong. It hurt Asteria."

My natural reaction was to reach out and hold my crying sister, but I knew better.

"It hurts when your husband doesn't understand why you don't want to have sex with him. It hurts when your husband puts his needs above your own. It hurts when your husband comes home with the stench of another woman's foul pussy on his face because he doesn't have the respect enough to wash himself after he fucks someone else! And it hurts to know that this was all my fault; had I'd never told Keith that he could have sex with other women this would not have happened."

I never felt sorrier for my sister than I did at that moment, but as much pain that she felt and as much as Keith has hurt her, I knew that she wouldn't leave him. "Pandia, maybe you and Keith should look into marital counseling to discuss the things that are going on in your relationship."

"Don't worry about my marriage; you need to worry about getting and keeping Latif a father in his life because Keith will never acknowledge him again." She fumed as she put her son's coat back on him.

"I am sorry for the pain that I caused you, I love you and I never meant to hurt you. This was not about you, it was about me. I was being selfish and I wanted to all, but the price that I paid was the cost of a relationship with my sister and for that I regret what I did. But remember Pandia, while you have every right to be pissed off at me, but keeping me and my son out of your life will not solve our marital problems. Keith is the issue and until he respects you and remains loyal to his marriage vows you will continue to have this problem. I was not the first one that Keith fucked and I guarantee that I won't be the last one."

"Have a nice, lonely life Asteria." Pandia said as she and her legitimate son walked out of my house.

45
SANTANA

I never knew the meaning to all cried out until the day Mike left me for good. Tabitha knew what she was doing all along; she got Keith's cell phone number out of my phone one night while I was sleeping. She went to Mr. Gold about our affair and told him that I was mistreating her after she ended things between the two of us to focus on her career with Gold's Medical Supply. After I demanded my credit card back she simultaneously sent the video to both Keith and I. I begged him to stay telling him that we could make our marriage work, but he wouldn't hear any of it. I kept replaying our last conversation in my head over and over again.

"We have built a life together let's not allow this one thing tear it all apart." I begged as he tossed his items in a packing box.

"I can't continue to sleep next to a wife who prefers the sexual gratification from another woman."

"I am sorry; I don't know why I did it…"

"If you can't figure out why you did it then how can you promise me that it is still not in you? How can you promise me that this will never happen again? How can you make the promise to me that every time a pretty woman walks by us you won't feel something deep down inside of you? PROMISE ME THAT!" Mike yelled in my face. Mike had never raised his voice at me, he was not raised that way, but this was something different.

"You don't understand," I cried, "I was lonely and confused. You would come home and ignore me night after night!"

"Why didn't you ever say anything to me about it?"

"I did Mike, but you don't listen."

"Then as my wife it is your job to make me listen not to start sleeping with a woman!" He turned his back to me so I wouldn't see the tears forming in his eyes.

"I tried."

"You didn't try, you ran." He sniffed "I love you with everything that God has given me to love with, but you betrayed me Santana. We have been together for so long, you have given me two beautiful children and I was a happy man. I didn't know how you were feeling, I guess that I didn't pay enough attention to you, but I never ran to the arms of another woman. I wouldn't have done you like that. I cannot lie next to you and pretend that this didn't happen because the pain is too much. I am sorry, but I am filing for a divorce in the morning." He put then he walked out of our bedroom wiping the tears from his eyes.

There was no more talking that I could do because Mike would never change his mind. I cannot believe that I allowed myself to be drawn into this world by Tabitha, but I cannot even blame her, it was my own-fault.

46
JOVANNA

Justin's mother was gone by the time I'd made it back home that afternoon. He was lying on the couch trying to watch television, but his wound made lying down on the stiff couch impossible.
"Hey." I smiled.
"Hey." He winced.
Walking over to him I knew what I had to do. "Come on let's get to bed honey, you will be more comfortable in there and you can watch a movie on my laptop." I offered as I helped my helpless fiancé off of the couch.
"Baby I am sorry about my mother, but you know how she can be." He said when I got him into bed.
"When was the last time that you had something for pain?" I asked him ignoring his last statement.
"This morning, mom gave me some Percocet."
"Justin that was over six hours ago." I fussed going into the bathroom to get him some water to drink with his medication.
Giving Justin the medication I cleaned his wound and changed the dressing, I wanted to cry at the large mark that Chad left on him, but he left an even larger mark on my life. The medication kicked in and Justin fell asleep. Ignoring my own pain I began cleaning our house and made

dinner only settling down to catch up on a few emails. Justin woke two hours later, it felt good to have him wrap his arms around me.

"Thank you Jovanna." He breathed.

"Thank you for what?"

"For being who you are and doing the things that you do."

I didn't say a word.

Justin kissed my neck softly as he caressed my breast, I moved his hand, and "Baby you are hurt." I protested.

"My gut his slashed, but everything else works just fine." He smiled as he continued to kiss me.

I rolled over to my back and gave Justin my tongue, "Doctor's orders are for you to take it easy."

"Then you get on top." He winked, "And I'll lay back and enjoy the ride."

I laughed.

"I love you Jovanna."

We looked silently into one another's eyes for a moment that seemed like eternity.

Justin broke the silence, "Now that we are about to be husband and wife and after all that we have been through over these past few months I need to know that I can trust you. I need to know that you are the woman who I have known all of this time and that I can lay next to you in bed and not have doubts in my mind." He said while holding my hand. "I might be a rich white boy, but I am also someone who has been there and done that so I am no fool."

I didn't know what to say; I'd never been honest about things with Justin. As far as he was concerned the run in with Chad was just some random act of violence as was the shooting. I was not woman enough to let my skeleton out of the closet for the fear of it ruining my relationship with the man that I was about to marry and for fear that when he looked at me the affection in his eyes would turn into affliction. I was not ready to be honest with him therefore I was not ready to be his wife.

"Justin as much as you and I have been through and throughout the adversity that has been made out of our union, honey I would be a fool to hide anything from you. You are my heart and soul, you know me better than anyone else knows me and I love you."

"The night that I lay bleeding on the ground, helpless, angry that I couldn't defend you against that man, I heard your conversation with him. He called you Marquita."

I gulped hard as the tears formed in my eyes, holding my head down I couldn't even look my man in his beautiful, blue eyes.

"At first I thought that he was a crazy man and this whole thing was a case of mistaken identity, but my thoughts have stayed with me this entire time and I know that this whole thing was not random. In the pit of my stomach I knew that you knew him and you knew who was tormenting us the whole time from the phone calls to the attack inside of our home. Are you hiding something from me?"

The tears escaped my eyes and fell onto my cheeks as I tried to continue the lie by shaking my head in denial.

"I followed you the day that you fell in the park and was confronted by that man in the Cadillac the same man that attacked us. I followed you to the pawn shops as you tried pawning the engagement ring that I brought you. I knew that you sold the engagement ring and the watch. I thought that you had a gambling addiction when you were found at the casino, but it just didn't add up. As angry as I was and as much as it hurt me to keep this all inside, I waited for you to finally come clean to me, but you failed me." Justin wiped tears from his eyes, "It bothers me that such an amazing woman could hide something from me that could have ended my life, all of the while looking me in my eyes and telling me that you love me every single night."

"You lied to me, you deceived me and now you want to marry me. Who am I marrying? Who are you?"

"I am Jovanna Justin." I cried, "I am the same woman that you nearly ran over in the park the day that we met, I am the same woman that you fell in love with and asked to marry you. I am me. Please trust that I have told you everything it is that you need to know about me."

Snatching away from me Justin lay back on his back, "I cannot marry someone that I do not know."

"Can't you just love who I am now Justin?" I asked, but he didn't answer, he only turned his back falling asleep.

The next morning I said the unthinkable to Justin as we lay on our own sides of the bed. "I can't do this." I said with tears in my eyes.

"Do what Jovanna?" Justin asked sitting upright in the bed.

"I don't think that I can marry someone who doesn't trust me."

"I never said that I didn't trust you."

"You did say that you didn't think that I was being honest with you about what has happened."

Justin scooted closer to me, wrapping his arms around me, but I pulled away from him, "I just don't understand what happened and yes I do think that you are keeping something from me, but it can't be something so bad that we can't work it out."

Getting up from the bed I put on a pair of lounge pants, "Some things are better left unsaid. Why can't you just leave well enough alone?"

"Because I want to know who in the hell that I'm marrying." He fumed. "You know all that there is to know about and if you want to know more then I will tell you. Why are you keeping secrets from me Jovanna?"

"I can't do this." I threw my hands up, "I am calling off the wedding."

Looking at me in disbelief and pain Justin managed to get out of bed, "Are you serious?"

"Baby lay back down before you injure yourself further."

"I am already injured Jovanna, but don't think that I'm about to let you just walk out of my life like this."

"There are some secrets that just need to be kept Justin."

"Not from your husband!" he fussed. "Did you kill someone or something?"

Slicing my eyes at him I walked out of the bedroom not only to get away from him and his constant questions, but also to hide my tears.

"Jovanna talk to me." He followed.

"There is nothing left to say; I just want out."

"What are you running from?"

"Trust me; I am doing you a favor."

Tears streamed down Justin's red face, "I don't understand what is happening to us. I love you so much; you said that you loved me, so why is it that you want to hurt me?"

"I don't want to hurt you and that is why I have to leave you." I turned towards him with tears streaming down my face, "Justin I love you too much to expose you to my skeletons. I want to be your perfect little Jovanna, but I am not perfect. I have secrets that would hurt your that is why I'd rather leave and hurt you now than wait around for you to be hurt later."

"Please Jovanna, don't go." He held onto my hand.

"I'm sorry." I said softly pulling away.

As hard as it was for me to walk away from a life that I loved and enjoyed, it would have been even harder to face the truth and tell Justin about my past.

Santana reveled her skeleton to Mike and it cost her the love and respect of her husband and her marriage. Asteria let her skeleton out of the closet, which ended up costing her the most important relationship that a woman can have, the relationship with her sister. I, on the other hand, was more comfortable with my secret hidden deep in my closet and now that Chad was gone for good this was a secret that would follow me to my grave, but as long as no one else knew about it I would never tell.

EPILOGUE
ASTERIA

I could hardly believe that it has been four months since I last spoke to Pandia and while I still thought about her and her son every day, I felt at peace to finally know that I was not caught up in a love triangle between her and Keith. It hurt when I had to give up my half of Gods & Goddesses, but it hurt even more have given up a relationship with my only sister.

Trying to end things with Eric was much harder than I thought that it would be. I thought that he would have wanted to leave me alone after I told him about Keith and I, but Eric was running from his own skeleton that he kept hidden in his closet. He'd moved from Florida three years after being released from a Florida prison for dealing drugs where he served eleven years of his life. After he was released from probation he moved to St. Louis where he and his cousin opened up the mechanic shop with hidden drug money that he had saved up before he went to prison.

"How can I judge you for what you did when what I did ruined families and changed neighborhoods?" He asked after telling me about his secret. "What you did was heinous, but you cannot live the rest of your life beating yourself up about the mistake that you made. You are seeking forgiveness from your sister, but who you really need forgiveness from is yourself."

Eric was right, I sent letters, flowers and cards to Pandia trying to get her to forgive me, but she never acknowledged them. The first month was the worst. I beat myself up on a daily basis because I felt that is what I deserved after what I'd done to my sister. However, after Eric and I talked about things I started to heal and finally I forgave myself. I hated the fact that Latif would not have his father in his life like he deserved, but he did have Eric who treated him like his own son.

It was odd seeing Santana living without Mike, but she was a lot happier. After the divorce was finalized she said that for the first time in a long time she felt free. She stopped going to church and began practicing Buddhism and she'd moved from the suburbs into a loft in the city. I knew that she still loved Mike, but now she loved herself even more. Although Mike got full custody of the children considering her drug use and the fact that he told the judge about the affair that she'd had with Tabitha, she was still able to see Malik and Mya for two weekends a month which seemed to make her happy.

Leaving Justin was one of the hardest things that Jovanna had to do, but no matter how much we tried to talk her out of it, she packed up her things and moved to Chesterfield. She told us that she couldn't bear to let Justin know about her past and she feared that he would never understand. I thought that if she'd told him he would have understood and forgave her. She was concerned more about his mother finding out and hating her even more for living down to the expectations that she'd set in place for Jovanna. After leaving she suffered from a bout of depression, had it not been for Santana and I she wouldn't have gotten the help that she needed from a local therapist to help cope with things instead of constantly running away.

I ran into Justin a few months after she left and while he was still hurt by her decision he was willing to try to work things out with her, but she wouldn't return any of his countless phone calls, emails and texts and she made us promise not to tell him where she moved to.

Skeletons live in everyone's closets, but it is when those skeletons start to come out that we lose focus on what is important as we try to keep those closet doors shut. It seems that it is easier to let the skeletons out and deal with issues of the past rather than fight to keep them hidden.

ABOUT THE AUTHOR

Shimeka is the mother of six children who resides in the small, but historic town of Alton, Illinois. She has been writing since the sixth grade and has always had a love affair of the written word having read anything from Dicken's to Dickey. She has been married to the love of her life for the past eight years and assures people that no more children will come of this blessed union. When Shimeka isn't writing, reading, wiping, cooking, fussing, yelling and cleaning she maintains her blog Six Kids & A Pen.

Shimeka R. McFadden

Made in the USA
Lexington, KY
28 October 2011